"Aunt Hope says you can't be our daddy."

His gaze swung back to Hope. "Did she, now?"

"Yeah." Harper took a quick, audible breath. "But she also said we can get a puppy instead."

"I said we'll see."

"Okay, yeah," Harper admitted, engaging Hope in a stare down. "But that's almost the same thing as yes."

Hope held the child's glare with an unflinching one of her own. "I made no promises, Harper."

Walker's chuckle interrupted the staring match. "Wise woman."

And now she was locked in a silent contest of wills with him. Their gazes held a long, silent beat. An unspoken message passed between them, but Hope couldn't quite decipher the meaning.

Walker broke eye contact first.

"Ready to move in to your new home?" The words were directed at the twins, but Hope felt them in the depths of her soul.

Eight words, spoken in that rich, masculine baritone, and the carefully constructed life she'd envisioned for herself with the twins morphed into something new. Something different.

And for the first time in her life, unrealized dreams seemed possible.

Renee Ryan grew up in a Florida beach town where she learned to surf, sort of. With a degree from FSU, she explored career opportunities at a Florida theme park and a modeling agency and even taught high school economics. She currently lives with her husband in Nebraska, and many have mistaken their overweight cat for a small bear. You may contact Renee at reneeryan.com, on Facebook or on Twitter, @reneeryanbooks.

Books by Renee Ryan

Love Inspired

Thunder Ridge

Surprise Christmas Family

Village Green

Claiming the Doctor's Heart
The Doctor's Christmas Wish

Love Inspired Historical

Charity House

The Marshal Takes a Bride
Hannah's Beau
Loving Bella
The Lawman Claims His Bride
Charity House Courtship
The Outlaw's Redemption
Finally a Bride

Visit the Author Profile page at Harlequin.com for more titles.

Surprise
Christmas Family

Renee Ryan

LOVE INSPIRED
INSPIRATIONAL ROMANCE

LOVE INSPIRED®
INSPIRATIONAL ROMANCE

ISBN-13: 978-1-335-55400-0

Surprise Christmas Family

Copyright © 2020 by Renee Halverson

This edition published by arrangement with Harlequin Books S.A.

For questions and comments about the quality of this book, please contact us at CustomerService@Harlequin.com.

Love Inspired
22 Adelaide St. West, 40th Floor
Toronto, Ontario M5H 4E3, Canada
www.Harlequin.com

Printed in U.S.A.

And he said unto me, My grace is sufficient
for thee: for my strength is made perfect
in weakness. Most gladly therefore
will I rather glory in my infirmities,
that the power of Christ may rest upon me.
—*2 Corinthians* 12:9

Chapter One

She was *not* stalking him, Hope Jeffries assured herself. Nothing so sneaky. She was simply confirming she'd found the right man. It was a risk, coming to his place of employment. But confronting him at a hospital was safer than showing up at his private residence.

Enough stalling. She was ready.

Hope unbuckled her seat belt, then checked her bag for the custody papers she'd had her attorney draw up last week. There they were, waiting for one final signature.

After a quick glance in the rearview mirror, she swiveled around to face the precious cargo sitting in the back seat. "Ready to go, girls?"

Two identical faces of dread stared back at her. Hope hated seeing the twins upset.

You're doing this for them.

For Harper and Kennedy. Her five-year-old

nieces had become her world. Hope desperately wanted to make their lives as easy as possible, especially after the ordeal of losing their mother to cancer barely three months ago. The Lord had given Hope an unexpected blessing out of tragedy. She would not squander this chance to do right by the sister she'd failed in so many ways.

"This won't take long." She increased the wattage on her smile by a million. "We'll be in and out in a flash."

Giving them no chance to argue, she climbed out of the rental car and stepped into Thunder Ridge, Colorado, founded in 1899. The sign at the edge of town claimed a population of 15,128 and an oxygen-stealing elevation of 9,111 feet.

For a moment, Hope simply stood there and drank in the scene. Wow, just…wow. The Christmas season had arrived with an explosion of sparkles and bright colors. Fat, lazy snowflakes fell over the heavily decorated buildings of Main Street. Wreaths adorned the old-world style streetlamps, while miles and miles of garland hung from every available ledge, roofline and storefront window.

"Beautiful," she whispered. It was as if she'd been dropped in the middle of a live-action postcard designed to lure tourists.

Hope was definitely lured.

Thunder Ridge was a far cry from New York

City. What must it be like to live here year-round? Pretty awesome, she guessed. The girls could be happy here. Hope prayed it didn't come to that.

I can't lose them, Lord. Her heart tripped at the thought. *I just can't.*

She might not have a choice.

Drawing in a deep, calming breath, she shifted her attention to the mountains looming on the horizon. They stood like dark, ominous guardians watching over what belonged to them. Hope could almost hear them say, "Intruder beware."

Now she was being fanciful. Dr. Hope Jeffries was never fanciful. As a college professor of Economics on track for tenure at Columbia University, she preferred practical theories to fairy tales.

One final look at the winter wonderland and she stepped back to the car. She helped the girls out of their car seats, then guided them onto the shoveled pavement of the hospital's parking lot.

"Let's do this." She used her most cheerful voice, remembering the advice their child psychologist had given Hope. Dr. Stephens had warned her that the girls took their cues from her.

Apparently not today. Instead of returning smiles, Hope received a chorus of pitiful sighs. Taking their tiny hands in hers, she steered the twins toward the sidewalk that led to the hospital's main entrance. They followed along in brooding silence.

"Aunt Hope? Do we *have* to go inside with you?" Kennedy glanced longingly over her shoulder, then shared a determined look with her sister. "Can't we wait in the car?"

"Absolutely not."

"If Mommy was here, she'd let us."

The disturbing thought had Hope gaping at her niece. "That can't possibly be true."

"It is so," Harper said. "We used to stay in the car all the time."

Hope prayed her niece was exaggerating. Surely Charity wouldn't have left her daughters in her beat-up VW Bug while she did, well, whatever called for her to fly solo. The possible activities were too numerous and, frankly, too frightening to contemplate. It was moments like these that Hope regretted the years of estrangement from her sister.

"Please, Aunt Hope," Kennedy whined. "Can't we sit in the car? You can lock us in. We won't try to get out. We know better."

"You're not waiting in the car."

"You might look like our Mommy," Harper said, hands on her hips. "But you don't act like her."

Her niece was correct. In terms of behavior, Hope had never been like her identical twin. There were times she wished she could be more carefree like Charity. Not this time. "You're coming with me, and that's the end of it."

Their crestfallen expressions nearly broke her heart. The twins had been through a lot of upheaval since Charity had shown up on Hope's doorstep. If this horrifying insight into their lives was true, their ordeal had started long before their mother had been diagnosed with breast cancer. *Oh, Charity, why didn't you come to me sooner?*

"Tell you what," she said, reaching for a compromise that would satisfy all three of them. "Once I'm finished with my—" she paused again "—errand, we'll stop in that sweetshop we passed this morning and get something fun to eat."

Kennedy's face lit up. "You mean, like, maybe some candy?"

"Maybe," Hope hedged, thinking a bribe probably wasn't the right way to go.

The girls looked at each other. In silent twin code, they communicated something only they understood, then nodded. "Okay," they said in unison.

Calling it a win, Hope squeezed each of their hands and set out for the hospital's entrance. She didn't like including the girls. She'd rather not have brought them to Colorado at all. But with their mother gone three months now, she was the only family they had left. Or rather the only family they knew.

That could change soon.

She wasn't ready.

What if Walker Evans wasn't a good guy? What if the private detective Hope had hired had missed something? The man had been pretty vague about the doctor's past, focusing mainly on the most recent few years.

This was a mistake.

Hope shouldn't have come to Thunder Ridge. She'd been too quick to act on her attorney's advice. She started to turn around, then stopped herself. She'd dragged the twins this far. She had to see this through. For their sake.

Keep telling yourself that. Admit it, professor, you're curious.

She was so curious.

How much did Walker Evans know about his daughters? She still fumed over the story Charity had told her right before she succumbed to the cancer. There'd been an impromptu Las Vegas wedding, and then a forced annulment when the selfish cad had discovered his new wife was pregnant. Hope couldn't imagine anyone being so heartless. She'd vowed to make him pay for what he'd done to her sister. Unfortunately, Charity died a handful of days after her confession, leaving Hope with more questions and very few answers.

She'd begun her search immediately following

Charity's funeral. How many Walker Evanses could there be? More than she would have expected, but she'd eventually found the right man. He was an emergency room doctor working the night shift at Thunder Ridge Hospital. He came from a large, close-knit family that included lots of siblings, several dogs and rambling houses with white picket fences.

Just then, she spotted Dr. Evans standing inside the emergency room's entrance.

Hope's feet ground to a halt. She'd found her man. Oh my…

His black hair curled at the tips, and those eyes, the shape so familiar, so similar to the ones that stared out of Harper and Kennedy's sweet faces. Hope swallowed back a ridiculous sigh as she watched him, head bent, speaking to a little boy with his arm in a sling. In full doctor-mode, he alternated his attention between the child and his parents, who responded with nods and smiles. Lots of smiles.

It was clear the man was well-liked. By at least three people.

Hope sorted through the mass of emotions raging through her. There was surprise, worry, a little awe and fear. So much fear, it brought a sting to the back of her eyes. Maybe he would decide to step up. Five years was plenty of time to change a mind.

Maybe she was being overly pessimistic. Maybe the man would sign over custody without a fight. He'd abandoned his pregnant wife. That spoke volumes about his character. Didn't it?

As if sensing her gaze on him, he wrapped up his conversation with the family, straightened to his full height of six foot three and turned his head in her direction. Their eyes met through the plate glass window. And…

Boom.

That's inconvenient, she thought.

She reminded herself that Harper and Kennedy were her first—her only—priority. And if all went according to plan, they would no longer be her nieces.

They would be her daughters.

Walker couldn't help noticing the woman lurking behind a large potted plant just outside the hospital's main entrance. Kind of hard not to notice her. She was looking straight at him. Her stare was unwavering, unfriendly and, if he were honest with himself, unsettling. He couldn't imagine what he'd done to warrant such blatant hostility from a complete stranger. He'd never met her before. He'd have remembered those almond-shaped eyes and all that wheat-colored hair hanging past her shoulders in thick, unruly waves.

His stomach did a fast, unexpected roll. He hadn't been this intrigued by a woman since...

He refused to let his mind finish the thought.

Still, the instant masculine interest was as unwelcome as it was unexpected. It made him feel itchy, sad and slightly empty inside. No, not today. He wasn't going to relive the past, not even in the privacy of his own thoughts. He shoved aside the agonizing memories clawing for release and focused on the woman glaring at him.

Locked in their silent battle of wills, he attempted a neutral smile.

Mystery woman did not return the gesture.

In fact, her spine straightened. It was obvious she didn't like him. *Really* didn't like him. People usually liked him. A good bedside manner was part of the job.

She moved past the plants, and...whoa. Walker's breath caught in his throat. Mystery woman was not alone. She had two very wide-eyed little girls with her. They were identical in size and coloring and were absolutely adorable.

Walker guessed the twins were somewhere around four, maybe five years old. They wore matching red coats with shiny gold buttons marching down the front. Plaid knit caps had been positioned over their sleek dark hair at a jaunty angle.

Something deep and miserable washed over

him. A familiar twinge of sorrow came next, giving him a hard pang in the center of his chest. Walker had come so close to happiness, and had actually had it for nearly a year, but then the Lord had cruelly ripped it away from him in a handful of hours. All that he had left was foggy memories, a lot of pain and something that had started as sorrow, but was becoming bitterness as each year passed.

He shook away the depressing insight as mother and daughters entered the building hand in hand in hand.

They drew closer, until Walker got a good look at the children's faces. His heart took another hit. Their eyes were a familiar pale blue. He'd seen those same eyes every day of his life. Whenever he looked in the mirror.

But that couldn't be.

The trio stopped a few feet in front of him. Walker rubbed a hand over his face, took another, longer look at the evidence staring back at him and accepted the truth.

The twins had his eyes.

Chapter Two

Hope witnessed the exact moment the good doctor made the family connection. The recognition was there in his frozen stance and stunned expression.

Clearly, she'd thrown him off balance. Or rather, the twins had. Hope had been right to approach him this morning.

As the man's gaze bounced from twin to twin, his shocked silence stretched into the uncomfortable. Shifted the power in Hope's favor. She pressed her advantage, reminding herself that this man might have—probably—abandoned his family. "Are you Dr. Evans? Dr. Walker Evans?"

She heard the disdain in her voice and nearly apologized. She wasn't usually so rude. But then she remembered what he'd done to her sister and, consequently, the twins. Hope had every reason to be antagonistic.

"That's right. I'm Dr. Evans. Are you, or—" with lightning speed, his gaze shifted from Harper to Kennedy, then settled back on Hope once again "—one of the girls, ill?"

"No, no. No!"

A faint smile crossed his lips. "One 'no' will do."

Hope frowned. She hadn't expected him to act so much like a, well, like a doctor. Then again, it was his profession. "The twins and I are perfectly healthy."

He visibly relaxed. In the next instant, he tensed up again. His body language wasn't guarded, exactly, but neither was it especially friendly. Did he recognize her, or rather—Charity?

"So," he began. "You're here because...?"

"I, that is, *we*..." Hope trailed off, not quite sure how to continue. Clearly, she hadn't prepared enough for this part of her plan. She'd expected recognition, denial, something. Anything but confusion.

"Okay. Let's try a different approach." He spoke with a gentle assertiveness that probably endeared him to his patients. "We've established who I am, and that none of you are sick, but I still don't know who you are or why you've come to my ER."

Right.

"I'm Hope. Hope *Jeffries*." She enunciated her

last name, waiting for some sign of recognition on his part.

None came, only more masculine bafflement that seemed a little too genuine to pass off as an act. It was possible Charity hadn't told him she had a twin sister, and so he wasn't making the connection. *Too many questions, not enough answers*, Hope thought. Or maybe he hadn't heard her clearly.

"Jeffries," she repeated.

Still nothing.

Something wasn't right. The man had married a woman with the same last name as Hope. Not just any woman, either, but Hope's identical twin. They shared matching features, except for a few cosmetic differences.

But no, not a single hint of recognition.

Hope considered her next move. She should probably introduce the twins. "This is Harper—" she touched the little girl's shoulder "—and this is Kennedy."

"Pleased to meet you, Miss Harper and Miss Kennedy." He smiled down at the girls with genuine warmth.

They grinned back.

"I have to say, you look very festive in your red coats," he said, clearly comfortable conversing with young children. "Santa would approve.

You can trust me on this. The jolly old man and I are friends."

"Really? You know Santa?"

"Absolutely."

Hope's lips twisted at a wry angle. She supposed his assertion wasn't a complete lie. He did dress up as the jolly old man every Christmas season at the homeless shelter. The investigator had given her that information with a smirk and eye roll.

"Santa and I spoke just the other day," he continued with a straight face. "It's a busy season for him, you know, but he always makes time for his friends."

The girls giggled, clearly charmed.

The feeling seemed mutual. Walker couldn't stop smiling at the twins. He remarked on their hats, which began an extensive dissertation from Harper, with occasional commentary from Kennedy, about their shopping trip to Macy's after the Thanksgiving parade.

As if mesmerized by the story, he leaned over, planted his hands on his knees and simply let the girls chatter away.

"Wow," he said when they wound down. "I can't imagine a better day. A parade *and* a shopping trip."

"Don't forget ice-skating," Kennedy reminded him. "We went ice-skating, too."

"Excellent." He swiveled his gaze up to Hope, stood tall and then stole her breath with a wink. "Well done."

Hope's plan was unraveling at her feet. The girls weren't supposed to warm up to their father so quickly. And he wasn't supposed to be putting them at ease with such effortless skill. Hope was debating how to wrestle back control of the situation when a gust of frigid air swept into the foyer.

"Why don't we get the three of you out of the cold?" Walker connected his gaze with Hope's. "And you can tell me why you're here."

"All right." Hope guided the girls deeper inside the building. She wasn't sure what she was going to say, or even do, but it didn't seem right to keep the twins standing in a draft while she decided her next step.

Battling a wave of doubt, she realized she needed to speak with the man alone.

As if reading her mind, he asked the twins, "Do either of you like to draw?"

"Not really." Harper responded for both girls. "But we like to color."

"Then you're in luck. We have coloring books and crayons in the first floor waiting room. Let's see if we can get you set up."

Five minutes later Walker had the twins sitting at a child-sized table, their coats on the back of their chairs, each with a coloring book and box of crayons in front of them.

"I'm going to have a quick word with your mother right in there." He pointed to a glassed-in room that overlooked the waiting area.

"But—" Kennedy's eyebrows scrunched together "—she's not—"

Hope cut off her niece with a quick shake of her head. "We won't be long."

"Okay." Shrugging, the girls went to work flipping through their individual books. Each stopped at a picture of a cartoon princess appearing in deep conversation with a frog.

As they began transforming the blank picture into colorful masterpieces, Hope took the lead. Walker followed close on her heels. Her stomach roiled at the mix of rubbing alcohol and antiseptic wafting around them. She hated that scent. It brought her back to Charity's final days. Why had she chosen a hospital for this confrontation?

The memory of her sister's fast decline hit Hope like a physical blow. She was instantly transported back to that cold, sanitized hospital room where the social worker told her it was time to call in hospice.

In a cruel twist of fate, the day she'd moved Charity into her apartment near the university had also been the girls' fifth birthday. Charity had rallied for the celebration, but all Hope could recall from that day was the bold red scarf wrapped around her sister's head and her thin, gaunt face.

Hope took in a breath. A mistake, as another dose of that horrible scent filled her nostrils. She lowered her head so her companion wouldn't see her reaction.

Once inside the glass-enclosed room, he wasted no time getting to the point. "Well, Hope *Jeffries*." He added the same emphasis on her last name as she'd used moments before. "You seem to know me, while I'm having a difficult time placing you. Tell me how we met."

"You don't remember?"

"Should I?"

She brushed the hair off her forehead, gave him a good, long look at her face and waited for him to make the connection. A heavy silence fell between them.

A beat passed. Then two. By the third, he crossed his arms over his chest and set a broad shoulder against the wall beside him. "So, we're back to that, are we? I have several skills, Mrs. Jeffries. Mind reading is not one of them."

"I'm not married." For some reason, she felt it important to correct him on that point.

He acknowledged this with a single nod. "All right, *Ms*. Jeffries. Who are you and want do you want from me?"

He was clearly losing patience with her. She was losing patience with herself.

"I thought…" She shook her head. "I wasn't expecting you to…" She broke off again, drew in a deep breath and tried again. "You really don't recognize my face?"

"Evidently, this is some sort of game for you." He dropped all signs of affability. "I'm at the end of a long shift and I'm not in the mood to play, so I'll ask again. Who are you?"

"You're asking the wrong question."

"What question should I be asking?"

She sighed. "It doesn't matter who I am, but rather who *they* are." She waved her hand in the general direction of the waiting room where the girls were absorbed in their coloring.

"All right." He studied the twins with a long, considering look. "Who are they?"

"You really can't guess?"

"So—" he shoved a hand through his hair "—we're back to the game-playing."

"I assure you, Dr. Evans, this is no game for me, or for the twins."

"Then tell me who they are."

"Harper and Kennedy are your daughters."

Walker resumed leaning against the wall, grinding his teeth in irritation and thinking cynically that Hope Jeffries had seemed so normal.

How had he failed to detect the crazy beneath that polished facade?

There was another possibility. Maybe this was some sort of prank one of his siblings had cooked up to shock him out of his predictable routine. All of them, except for his brother working in Africa, had been pushing Walker to join the living again, even going so far as to insist he shake things up a bit.

He was sufficiently shaken.

"Who sent you?"

"No one sent me." She blinked rapidly, and if he wasn't mistaken, tears were welling up in her eyes, almost as if he'd offended her with his question.

Walker wasn't buying the innocent act.

Her claim was too ridiculous to be real, not to mention impossible. He would remember fathering twins. No one was that forgetful. Thinking through her potential collaborators, he decided his oldest sister was the most likely candidate. "Did Quinn put you up to this?"

"I don't know anyone named Quinn." She said this without making direct eye contact.

Walker narrowed his eyes. "Remy?"

"I assure you, Dr. Evans, no one *put me up* to this." Her lips flattened in a grim line. "I sought you out this morning with one goal in mind. To introduce you to your daughters."

Walker shook his head. His mother had been wild about soap operas. Any child growing up in her home had been forced to watch the ridiculous shows a time or two. Walker knew this particular story line. A beautiful, mysterious stranger—she was always beautiful and mysterious—arrives in town claiming one of the male leads fathered her child. Amnesia was often a secondary plotline.

The situation was almost comical.

Except, Walker was not amused. "You've had your fun, Ms. Jeffries, but your little joke has gone on long enough."

"I did not travel all this way to make a joke." Her manner stopped just short of combative.

Walker was feeling fairly antagonistic himself. "Then why are you here?"

"I told you."

He attempted to stare a lie out of her.

She held steady under his gaze, not a flinch, barely a blink. Oh, she was good.

A very unpleasant thought occurred to Walker. This woman seemed to have intimate knowledge of his routine, enough to know where he would be this morning. Granted, he was a creature of habit. Anyone could figure out his schedule after minimal observation. Clearly, Ms. Jeffries had been watching him, following him, or had hired someone for the task.

Alarming, to say the least.

He should be afraid. But for some inexplicable reason he wasn't. He was, however, furious she'd targeted him. The woman was about to learn that Walker Evans was no easy mark.

He went on the offense. "How long have you been stalking me?"

"I have not been stalking you."

"No?" He pushed from the wall and moved to tower over her. Not hard to do. She was a good five inches shorter. "You somehow found out where I work and the hours I clock in and out on a regular basis. Then, you show up at the end of my shift so that you could make this ridiculous claim. That is, by its very definition, stalking."

"I suppose, from your point of view, it would seem that way."

"You…*suppose*?" The word came out in an angry growl. It took all his willpower not to walk her out of the building. "What would you call it?"

Her attention dropped to the floor, but not before Walker saw the sliver of guilt moving through her gaze. "There was nothing sketchy about my behavior."

"Only all of it."

"All right, yes, I made it my business to discover as much as I could about you. I did it for the twins' sake." She jerked her head up, looking as fierce as any mother he'd met through the years. "They are my first—my *only*—priority."

She genuinely appeared to care for the girls. Walker was almost impressed. Almost, but not quite. "Not sure teaching them how to stalk a man is in their best interest. Notice how I keep using that word. *Stalk.*"

Instead of backing down, she reacted with a show of temper. "Try to look at this from my perspective. I needed to know if you were worthy of meeting Harper and Kennedy."

"Those girls are not my daughters." He couldn't put a fine enough point on that.

Mouth grim, she pivoted to look out into the waiting room. Pressing her palm flat against the wall of glass, she sighed heavily, then dropped her hand by her side. "This isn't how our conversation was supposed to go."

"What did you expect? Did you think you could just show up here, make your outrageous claim and then have me fall in line because the twins and I share the same eye color?"

"The resemblance is much stronger than that."

He didn't disagree. But Walker knew better than to say as much. "How did you pick me? No, let me guess. You did a Google search for men with dark hair, blue eyes and a healthy bank account."

"This is not about money."

Walker frowned at the sight of those two adorable little girls coloring with focused resolve.

Their tiny, identical scowls reminded him of his brother Brent at that age, so determined, so focused on their task. He detected a hint of sadness about them, too, and that just slayed him.

They were sweet and innocent, and nothing like their scheming mother. Walker felt a pang of sorrow for the girls, wishing, in that moment, that they really were his daughters. He'd nearly been a father once. The Lord had taken that from him, as well.

Walker hardened his heart and turned to their mother. "How long did it take you to find a man that looked enough like the twins to put your scam into motion?"

"You want to know how I found you? I did an internet search. And, yes, I used Google. I also hired a private detective to fill in the blanks."

"You...wait, what? You hired a private detective?" Shocked into momentary silence, Walker stared at her. The woman really was crazy. How else could he explain hiring an investigator to zero in on her mark? Had she chosen Walker because he was a lonely widower who buried his grief in work, work and then even more work?

That seemed overly cruel. Something didn't add up here, something that kept nagging at the back of his brain. "Why me?"

"Harper and Kennedy deserve to know their father, and before you start denying you're him—"

she swung her purse off her shoulder "—I have proof."

Other than a DNA test, maybe a pair of birth certificates, which couldn't possibly exist, there was nothing she could show Walker that would corroborate her absurd claim. "All right, I'll bite. Show me this so-called proof."

"Gladly." With a jerk of her wrist, she unzipped the black bag, rummaged around, then pulled out a thin manila folder. "Here. What do you have to say for yourself now?"

Walker took the document she shoved into his hand and lowered his head. "It's a marriage certificate, issued on—" he recited a date not quite six years ago "—by the state of Nevada."

"The ceremony was conducted in a Las Vegas wedding chapel."

Las Vegas? How did the Marriage Capital of the World play into her scam?

"Take a look at the signature right there." She jabbed her finger at the groom's name, her palm covering the area where the bride had signed.

Walker blinked at the sight of his own name scrawled in a bold, familiar flourish. Where had he seen that handwriting?

"That's my name. But not my signature." He set the certificate on a nearby table. "Your private detective steered you to the wrong man."

"How many Walker Bartholomew Evans do you think there are in North America?"

"No idea."

"Seven."

"So many?"

"The groom claimed he was an ER doctor. You are the only medical doctor with your same name."

"Let me point out, Ms. Jeffries, the large flaw in your story." Walker kept his voice measured, although he was feeling anything but calm. "I've never been to Las Vegas."

He'd married Rachel surrounded by two hundred of their closest family and friends at Thunder Ridge Community Church. The day had been bright and sunny, the perfect start to the rest of their lives. Walker had been full of optimism. He'd said his vows in front of God, naively believing He would bless the marriage for many years to come.

"Now you're just being difficult, Dr. Evans. Take a look at this." She reached inside the folder again. This time, she pulled out an 8x10 glossy photograph. "Visual proof you were in Las Vegas at the time of the wedding."

Walker studied the image of a smiling couple surrounded by large urns overflowing with ugly, plastic flower arrangements. The bride bore a remarkable likeness to the woman glaring at him.

There were differences, most of which could be explained away by the passage of time. There was another explanation, of course, but that conversation was for later.

For now, Walker switched his attention to the groom.

A knot of disappointment tangled in his gut. What had possessed Brent to participate in a tacky Las Vegas wedding?

And, yeah, there was no denying the groom was Brent, grinning like a loon, eyes suspiciously unfocused. He stood next to an equally glassy-eyed woman that resembled Hope Jeffries, and yet not really. Walker bounced his gaze between the flesh-and-blood woman glaring at him and the bride in the photo.

He reached for the marriage certificate again, snatching it up before she could object, and studied the bride's signature. *Charity Jeffries.*

Well, well, well.

His unexpected visitor wasn't crazy, after all.

Walker couldn't say the same for his brother. What had Brent been thinking, signing Walker's name instead of his own on a marriage license?

It seemed unnecessarily petty, even considering their strained relationship at the time.

What had Brent hoped to gain?

He'd lost far more than he'd won by sticking it to Walker, namely five years as a father to those beautiful little girls. Walker glanced at the duo, looked back at the date on the certificate. "When did you say the twins were born?"

"They turned five in July of this year."

"What day?"

"The tenth."

Walker did the math. Harper and Kennedy had arrived in the world exactly forty-one weeks and three days following Brent's marriage to Charity. The numbers added up.

Setting aside the document, he watched the girls through the glass. Even the way they colored reminded Walker of his brother. It wasn't out of the realm of possibility that Brent had had a quickie Vegas wedding. But to marry a woman, then abandon her and their daughters? That wasn't in his brother's DNA. Speaking of DNA, although Walker didn't doubt Brent was the father of those precious girls, a test would have to be taken to prove paternity.

Before all that, Brent had some serious explaining to do.

Walker returned his attention to the wedding picture. He thought back to the year listed on the marriage certificate. His brother had experienced unspeakable tragedy, which could explain his erratic behavior and bad choices.

"Well?" Hope's voice brought Walker back to

the immediate problem at hand. "Do you still deny paternity?"

"I take it you have birth certificates, as well?"

She looked away. "Of course."

"That's not me in the photograph."

And that wasn't her in the picture, either. Which brought up a host of questions that Walker decided to save until they'd sorted out this unfortunate case of mistaken identity. "Wait here."

"You're *leaving*?" She sounded as outraged as she looked, all wide-eyed and furious. "Just like that?"

"I'm not leaving. I have something tucked away in my cubicle that you need to see. I would take you with me, but one of us has to stay here and watch the girls."

She glanced at the twins, then back at him, her eyes wary. "I don't think it's a good idea to let you—"

"Trust me." He touched her arm, willing her to see that he, unlike her, never lied. And he certainly didn't play games. "You're going to want to see this."

Her eyebrows slammed together. "What could you possibly have to show me?"

"Proof that I'm not the twins' father."

Chapter Three

Hope stared after Walker's retreating back, a sharp pain in her heart, the sensation cinching tighter and tighter. She wasn't an anxious person by nature, but she couldn't seem to stand still while he retrieved his supposed proof. She paced in a circle, wondering, worrying and wanting to jump out of her own skin. She had the right man.

He was the girls' father. Her proof was solid. What sort of evidence could he have that would possibly refute hers?

She paused at the plate glass window. The twins were completely absorbed in their task, heads bent in deep concentration, totally unaware of the drama playing out between their father and aunt.

The vice around her heart tightened. Hope loved Harper and Kennedy as if they were her own. The emotion ran deep, all the way down to the cellular level. If Walker didn't want them in his life, no problem, she wasn't here to change his mind. She would happily adopt them and take them back to New York. All she needed was his notarized signature on the custody papers.

When it came to family, the twins were all she had now.

Please, Lord, let him give them to me without a fight.

For a prayer, it wasn't especially wordy. Admittedly, she was rusty. She hadn't prayed since Charity died. The Lord had remained silent then. Maybe he wouldn't answer this time, either.

No use making assumptions. Hope was not giving up her quest for custody, and that was that. She would hound Walker until he admitted he was the twins' father. She would get him to sign over custody and continue on with her life free of guilt, knowing she'd done the right thing by coming here.

The masculine clearing of a throat announced his return.

With renewed resolve, Hope spun around to face him. What she saw surprised her. His eyes were filled with silent apology and a surprising amount of commiseration. An infuriating combination. Hope immediately bristled, dropping her gaze before he could see her reaction. It was only then that she noticed he held a silver picture frame in his hand.

"What's that?"

"A family portrait." He pressed the frame in her hands. "Take a look."

Her fingers automatically curled around the cold metal. "I don't see what a family picture has to do—"

"Look at the photograph, really look, then we'll talk."

Frowning, she studied the outdoor image of four men, brothers clearly, and two women, obviously their sisters. The siblings had been caught in a casual moment, appearing more candid than posed.

As the insanely gorgeous faces smiled at her, Hope's heart filled with a mix of dread and longing. Respect. Love. Support. She could see it all written in the collective body language. Unmistakable affection was there as well, in the positioning of hands randomly set on shoulders or arms slung around waists. The very essence of family had been captured in a single click of the camera's shutter and was too genuine to be explained away by chance.

Panic lodged in Hope's throat, stealing her ability to breathe.

The twins were related to these people. They were their family.

I'm going to lose them.

She couldn't bear the thought.

"Take a closer look at the people in the picture. That's me," Walker said, "right there, in the middle. The man on my right is Casey. He's the oldest and is a former military pilot with his own private cargo company. He also owns a coffee shop in town." He let that sink in a minute before adding, "The man on Casey's left is McCoy, a local photographer and artist. That's Quinn." He pointed to the taller of the two women. "She owns a sweetshop and tearoom in town. Our sister Remy is a veterinarian."

Quinn and Remy, the people he'd assumed had sent Hope to play a joke on him. The Evans siblings felt comfortable enough to play pranks on one another. Something moved deep inside her, a yearning so strong her knees threatened to buckle.

The twins were a part of this large, happy family. They belonged to them.

Hope had never belonged to anyone. Her father hadn't wanted her or Charity after their mother died, instead choosing to travel as a missionary to the Middle East. Even her sister hadn't wanted a relationship with Hope, saying she was too hung up on rules to be any fun. She'd spent her entire life on the outside looking in, always wishing for something just out of reach.

"And, finally," Walker said, still guiding her

through the photograph, "the man on the far left, there—" he placed his fingertip on the image and tapped twice "—that's my brother Brent. Take a good, long look at him."

Hope did as he instructed, a sick feeling in the pit of her stomach.

"Brent—" Walker tapped the image again "—is the man you're looking for."

"But—" Hope swallowed "—your name is on the marriage certificate."

"I have no idea why my brother signed my name instead of his own. And believe me, he will answer for his behavior." He tried to take the picture. Hope held on to it and continued focusing on Brent Evans. "My brother is the man in the wedding photograph, not me. Brent is the father of your twins."

Her cheeks burned hot with humiliation. She'd made a colossal error. "I don't know what to say."

"It was a logical mistake," he allowed. "Brent and I are only eighteen months apart. We look a lot alike, and—"

"—could be twins."

He acknowledged this with a nod. "Others have said the same. But if you look closely, there are obvious differences."

She saw them now. Walker was taller by an inch and a half, maybe two. He was slightly leaner in build. His hair had more wave. Brent had a small scar over his left eye. There were more, but she didn't need to catalog them to know she'd made a terrible error in judgment.

Hope considered herself a practical woman. She could admit when she made a mistake. And she'd just made a big one. She returned the picture and said, "I was wrong."

"Yes, you were."

"In my defense, the evidence was strong."

"Except for one glaring detail." His voice held a note of censure.

Hope prickled. "How was I supposed to know your brother signed your name?"

"Now who's being difficult, *Ms*. Jeffries? I'm referring to something more obvious. You bore Brent's children. You had to know I wasn't the right man on first sight."

Hope sighed. Time to come clean. "I'm not the twins' mother."

"I figured that out already."

"Their mother was my identical twin sister."

"Yep, figured that one out, as well." His lips twisted at a sardonic angle. "Why not admit the truth at the beginning of our meeting? Why lie?"

"I didn't lie, exactly."

"A lie by omission is still a lie. Or as my brother-in-law is fond of saying, a half-truth is a whole lie."

Walker's brother-in-law wasn't wrong. Hope

could feel the girls slipping away from her. Harper and Kennedy had uncles and aunts and cousins. What could she offer that compared to a large, extended family?

Her unconditional love and stability and so much more. This wasn't over.

"You led me to believe you were their mother."

She started to argue. But in the next breath, the fight left her. "I was wrong to do that."

How many times would she have to say that to gain absolution? As many as it took, she decided, knowing she had to make this right for the twins.

"We finally agree on something." She expected him to give her a much-deserved lecture. But instead, he added, "I prefer we were on the same page going forward, as well."

"Me, too." She meant every word.

He gave her a wide, boyish grin.

That smile. It made the man appear even more approachable than before, and really, really likeable. Hope didn't want to like Walker Evans. Technically, he was still the enemy.

What must he think of her?

She'd come to Thunder Ridge, guns blazing, making her accusations and…wait. So, she'd confronted the wrong Dr. Evans. Nothing had really changed, had it? The twins' father had walked away from his pregnant wife. Hope could still win custody. All she needed was a legally binding, notarized signature from Brent Evans and probably a DNA test. She needed to call her lawyer.

She also needed to speak with Brent Evans. "Would you be willing to introduce me to the twins' father?"

His smile dropped. "That's going to be a problem."

"Dr. Evans, please—"

"Call me Walker."

She nodded. "Walker, won't you reconsider?"

"You don't understand. It's not that I don't *want* to introduce the twins to Brent." He took her hand, gave it a gentle squeeze, held on. "It's that I *can't*."

Hope didn't want to be soothed by Walker's touch. But she was. "I...don't understand." And then she thought that maybe she did. "Is he incapacitated, or...ill?"

Were the twins about to lose another parent? The Lord couldn't be that cruel.

"It's nothing like that. Brent is fine. Unfortunately, he's currently out of the country."

"Is he on vacation?" she queried.

"It's a bit more honorable than that." Walker gave her hand another squeeze. "Brent is in Africa working for Doctors Without Borders."

The twins' father was in Africa? Dumbfounded by Walker's revelation, Hope clenched her jaw so hard her teeth ached from the pressure. It was too much to believe, and yet too ludicrous to be anything but true.

Africa. The word swirled around in her brain, nagging at her, shaming her for all the ugly thoughts she'd had about Walker Evans—a man who volunteered at a homeless shelter—and his brother, a man working for an international humanitarian organization. Both would look better in front of a judge in family court than a single woman with no family who taught Economics in New York City at a fancy private college.

Of all the scenarios Hope had conjured in her mind, learning that their father was working for Doctors Without Borders didn't make the top ten. It hadn't even made the list.

I'm going to lose the girls.

She breathed in slowly, catching a whiff of antiseptic that was uncomfortably strong. For a shocking moment, she thought she was going to be sick.

Hold it together.

The effort drained Hope of any remaining scraps of dignity. Images of Brent Evans administering medical care to the sick and impoverished sent another jolt of shame through her. Fear soon followed. Would a man like that openly deny his daughters?

Possibly. Her own father had done just that.

Hope's surroundings slowly came into focus, and she realized Walker still held her hand. His touch speared warmth up her arm and slammed into her heart. She should free her hand from his grip. She couldn't seem to move. The physical connection grounded her.

Frustration, urgency, embarrassment—the emotions knotted inside her. All those hours of research and the money spent on a private detective had brought her no closer to adopting her nieces.

"I see I've rendered you speechless." Walker's voice lacked any sign of condemnation. One more piece of evidence that proved he was the better person.

Hope shut her eyes a moment, wincing at the thought of her open hostility. "I don't know what to say—" she opened her eyes "—except I'm sorry for how I approached you."

"No worries." His blue eyes filled with compassion and understanding. It was the kind of look Hope had received from her sister's doctors whenever they presented bad news.

Walker Evans must be really great with his patients. Hope had to look away to catch her breath. When she returned her gaze, he was smiling, softly, kindly. The grain of black stubble on his jaw only managed to make him seem more approachable. Not some superhero with a medical degree. Just a regular guy with a bit more training than most men.

He let go of her hand.

The lack of contact left her feeling empty.

"If it helps," he said, taking a small step back, "I'm experiencing my own shock over the situation. I can't begin to imagine what was in my brother's head six years ago." Something in his gaze said he had a few guesses.

Hope would like to hear them. But first, she had her own admission to make. "I could say the same for my sister." Had her sister been completely honest with her about the twins' father? "Charity and I really never understood each other."

"An oddity for identical twins."

Hope didn't disagree. She and Charity had always been one step off. Yes, they'd been sisters, siblings, but never really close. "There was love between us, of course. It's just, our personalities were so different. We never had that twin connection I see in Harper and Kennedy."

Walker glanced at the wedding photograph, then looked back at Hope. "Now that, I believe."

They shared a smile, Hope's far more somber than the one Walker wore. She closed her eyes and sighed, regretting *so* much.

How she missed her sister and all the lost years they could never get back. The previous eight months had passed too quickly. The focus had been on Charity's illness and taking care of the twins rather than restoring their fractured relationship. Honest conversations had been rare. They'd made amends, but there hadn't been enough time to reconcile completely. Again, Hope wondered if Charity had been completely forthright about the twins' father.

She hated doubting her sister when Charity wasn't able to defend herself.

Sighing, Hope touched the photograph, carefully tracing the woman who was the polar opposite of her in every way but looks. "Everyone adored Charity. She was the outgoing twin."

She'd been almost childlike in her need for fun, perhaps even thoughtless in her pursuit of a good time. But Charity had brought Harper and Kennedy into the world when she could have made other choices.

For that alone, Hope could forgive her sister any mistakes she made as a mother. "Your brother and my sister made two beautiful children."

"I couldn't agree more. Look at that." Walker waggled his finger in the space between them. "We've agreed a second time. If we keep this up, we might actually become friends."

Hope's cheeks heated at the lighthearted comment. "I wouldn't go that far."

He chuckled.

Her heart pinged.

What would it be like to call this man a friend? It wasn't out of the realm of possibility. Their lives were connected now, tethered by two gorgeous little girls born three days, one week and nine months after a spontaneous Las Vegas wedding.

"The twins have been through a lot of turmoil in their short lives." Shifting slightly, she watched them. They were still coloring, but the squirming had begun. Hope calculated five minutes more and they would come looking for her. And she was only a smidge closer to finding their father. "What am I going to do?"

"Now who's asking the wrong question?"

"I'm sorry?"

"The question is…what are *we* going to do?" Walker stepped closer. Hope could feel his heat rolling over her like a warm, healing summer breeze. "I'm not your enemy, Hope. We're in this together."

And just like that, her resentment evaporated, replaced by an odd thrill of something she couldn't quite pinpoint. Relief, maybe? She might be back at square one, but she wasn't alone anymore. It was an unfamiliar, heady feeling, and one she didn't dare trust.

"I have to wonder why you came looking for

the twins' father alone. Why didn't your sister join you?"

Hope started at the question, then realized Walker didn't know Charity was dead.

"I'm assuming something happened to her."

The man was perceptive. Under different circumstances, Hope would consider that an attractive character trait, but now it only made her sad. "My sister died recently."

His face softened in sympathy. "I'm sorry."

She was painfully aware that those two, simple words were exactly what she needed to hear. Had Walker offered empty platitudes, Hope would have closed herself off completely. But her usual defenses were crumbling under his gentle manner.

"How did she die?"

She hadn't spoken of Charity's passing with anyone besides the girls, and even then only in the most careful, gentle way.

Had Hope been feeling less wretched over the way she'd approached Walker, she would have brushed aside his question. Instead, she found herself saying, "She died of breast cancer three months ago."

"That's rough." Walker said nothing more, probably waiting for her to continue. At least he didn't attempt to touch her again.

"Charity showed up on my doorstep this past

February, her daughters in tow. Until that day, I had no idea she was a mother."

"None?"

She looked away, feeling the guilt all over again. Why hadn't she tried to contact her sister through the years? Why had she allowed Charity to hold a grudge over who-knew-what? Hope still didn't know what had possessed her sister to cut all ties with her.

"We'd been estranged for years," she admitted. "Every one of which melted away the moment I laid eyes on her. She looked so beat down. When she shared the terrible news of her diagnosis, I never thought the cancer would be fatal."

"I'm sorry." Walker touched her then, nothing more than a brush of his fingertips across the back of her hand. The need to lean on him was a jolt Hope felt all the way down to her toes.

If she gave in to it, she would shatter.

"I could give you all sorts of clichés to ease your pain," he said, quickly looking away, swallowing a few times, as if trying to pull himself together. Then, blinking rapidly, he glanced back at her, deep sadness swirling in his gaze. "But there are some losses words never heal."

He sounded as if he spoke from personal experience. Had he lost someone he loved? The private investigator hadn't mentioned anything about a death of a spouse or girlfriend. Hope was coming to realize he hadn't been as thorough as she'd paid him to be, as evidenced by her approaching the wrong man. And now this, the genuine understanding that seemed far too real to be fake.

"Thank you." Her voice sounded as broken as she felt.

This man was a stranger, but a sympathetic one. He was also a man with a shared stake in the situation. The twins were his nieces, too. This moment of solidarity could very easily turn adversarial if she wasn't careful.

Hope needed Walker as an ally. Perhaps if she appealed to the healer in him, he would work with her.

"The doctors discovered the cancer too late. It all happened so quickly." Now that she started, the words spilled out of her in a rush. "After years of no communication, not even a text, there she was, on my doorstep, my sister. My twin. Asking me for help. I welcomed her back into my life without question. And her daughters. Harper and Kennedy are—"

"Hold that thought." Walker's sudden interruption had her nearly choking on her words. His quick "Hey, kiddos" shook Hope to the core.

How much had they heard?

Moving quickly, she rushed forward and dropped in front of them. "Perfect timing." She smoothed her expression into a pleasant smile. "We're just finishing up."

Neither girl responded. They were too busy staring up at Walker, eyes wide with adoration. Hope couldn't blame them. He'd turned his smile on the children and, well, *wow*. The man had a killer smile. Hope's heart lifted, sighed.

"What's that?" Kennedy pointed up to his neck.

"What? This old thing?" His smile turned into a playful grin. "It's called a stethoscope."

"The doctors used one of those on my mom." Harper studied the instrument with keen interest. "We weren't allowed to touch it, not ever."

"You can touch this one." Walker unwrapped the instrument from around his neck and lowered to his haunches. "It's used for listening to heartbeats. Go on. Touch it." He held the instrument closer to the girls. "You won't break it."

Both reached out tentatively. Harper's hand touched the black tubes first. Kennedy's followed a second later.

"These are the earpieces." Walker pointed to the identical ends. "They go into your—"

"Ears!" the girls shouted simultaneously.

"Exactly, and this is the chest-piece."

"That goes on your heart," Harper told him with no small amount of pride.

"Right again. Want to take a quick listen?"

Two pairs of eyes swung up to Hope. "Can we?"

"Of course."

"Who wants to go first?"

Kennedy answered a split second before her sister. "Me."

"Okay." Walker placed the earpieces in the girl's ears. "Can you hear my heartbeat? It sounds like lub-dub, lub-dub, lub-dub."

"I hear it!" Kennedy shouted the words.

"I want to try." Harper bounced on her toes. "Let me try."

Walker gave the excited child a turn.

With a sinking sensation in the pit of her stomach, Hope watched the interaction between uncle and nieces. Walker was really good with the girls. It had taken Hope weeks to win them over like that.

To be fair, she'd never been around children before Charity had shown up on her doorstep. Dr. Stephens had assured Hope that a bit of awkwardness was to be expected.

She was being too hard on herself. What did it matter how she and the twins had started? They were close now. For all intents and purposes, she was their mother.

Lesson over, Walker wrapped the stethoscope back around his own neck.

Now that the ice had been broken, Harper and Kennedy couldn't stop talking. The conversation turned to one of their favorite topics since arriving in Thunder Ridge. "Do you know how to build a snowman?"

"Do I know how to build a snowman?" Walker's voice held a note of amused irony. "You, my little friend, are in the presence of a master craftsman."

"Really?"

"I have skills, kiddo, taught to me by my older brother, a man world-renowned for his ice sculptures."

"I bet I'm better," Kennedy said, her little chin lifted at a proud angle.

Hope blinked at her niece. Kennedy knew how to build snowmen? That was news to her. With Charity's illness, then the onslaught of the summer months, and then setting the girls up in school, there hadn't been much time for playing in the snow. Okay, none.

"I like your confidence, kid." Walker patted Kennedy on the shoulder.

"I'm good, too," Harper said, rushing to stand next Kennedy, nearly knocking over her sister in the process. "I'm even better than her."

The girls scowled at each other. A little pushing ensued. Before full-on mutiny broke out, Walker smoothly stepped between them. Shifting them apart with a gentle nudge on each of their shoulders, he eyed the girls with a mix of amusement and affection. "There's a way to settle this."

Again, the girls spoke as one. "How?"

"We build a snowman."

"Can we do it now?"

"Now could be a problem." Walker made a grand show of looking around him, his movements exaggerated. "I'm currently out of snow."

Harper giggled. "Not here, silly."

"Well, we do have a park at the center of town with lots and lots of the white stuff." He swiveled a questioning gaze at Hope. "You game?"

He wanted to build a snowman, now? As in, this morning? "I was thinking we would touch base with your brother first. Then, maybe, you know—" she shrugged "—go from there."

"Ah." Walker checked the chunky watch on his wrist. "It's the middle of the afternoon in Zimbabwe. He may be out in the field or in surgery or, well, you get the idea."

"Oh." She couldn't keep the disappointment out of her voice.

"Tell you what, I'll send a quick text asking him to get in touch with me, stat."

Hope breathed a sigh of relief. "I would really appreciate that."

"Okay." There was a moment of hesitation, but then he pulled out his cell phone and began tapping on the screen. His thumbs worked at lightning speed. He paused, studied the phone, then went back to typing out his message.

At last, he looked up. "Want to take a look before I press send?"

"Please."

He handed Hope the phone. She lowered her head, read quickly. The message was short and to the point.

Brent, we need to talk ASAP. A situation has arisen that requires your immediate attention.

"A—" Hope glanced at the girls "—situation?"

Walker followed the direction of her gaze. "Some things are better not put in a text."

He was right, of course. But still. Harper and Kennedy were too precious to be summed up as a *situation*.

"Hope." Walker touched her shoulder. "Do you have a revision you'd like to make?"

She reread the text, shook her head. "No." She handed over the phone. "It's good."

"Okay." Eyes never leaving hers, Walker touched the screen. An electronic whooshing sound indicated the text had been sent. "Now, we wait."

"We wait."

They continued staring at each other, neither moving, neither looking away.

"In the meantime—" A slow smile spread across Walker's face. Oh, that smile. "—what do you say we build a snowman?"

Hope sighed. Spending the morning in a field of snow with the twins' uncle wasn't a terrible idea. It would give her a chance to get to know Walker better, maybe get some information about his brother.

What could possibly go wrong?

"Sure. Let's do it."

Chapter Four

Walker went through a dozen emotions before settling on relief. The appearance of Hope and the twins meant he wouldn't have to fill his morning with frantic activity in an effort to forget. He wouldn't have to trudge home to an empty house or pray exhaustion took over before memories flooded his mind.

There were days when he found them comforting, but mostly they just made him sad. His family was right. He needed to let Rachel go. To what end? Peace of mind, yes, but who would remember her if not him? She'd been an orphan. No parents, no siblings, only Walker. He couldn't let her death relegate her to obscurity.

Shaking off a rush of melancholy, he put on a brave face and escorted the Jeffries back the way they came. The automatic doors slid open and the four of them stepped into the crisp Colorado morning air. The twins kept up an excited chatter. Their aunt remained silent, even when Harper asked if they could stop for hot chocolate before playing in the snow.

The suggestion gave Walker an idea, one that would make next steps go smoothly, at least for him. "I know just the place. Quinn's Sweet Shop is a block off the park."

"Quinn?" Hope's face scrunched in concentration, as if trying to remember where she'd heard the name. "Oh, Quinn. The older of your two sisters, the business owner not the vet."

"That's her." He gave Hope what he hoped was a nonthreatening smile. "The shop won't be open yet, but she'll be there. I'll give her a quick call to let her know we're coming. If you get there before me, knock on the front door. She'll let you in."

One of the girls stopped him with a tug on his arm. "You're not riding in our car?"

"I have a few things to finish up here first." Her little face fell and to Walker's horror, she looked like she was about to cry. "Hey, now, Kennedy, I'll be there. I promise."

She sniffled then, eyes wide, angled her head slightly to the left. "You know I'm Kennedy?"

"Well, sure."

"Most people can't tell us apart." This, from Harper, with equal amounts of awe.

Walker couldn't help but point out the obvious. "You, my little friend, will soon learn I'm not most people."

Time to start the process of bringing Harper and Kennedy into the Evans family fold. "I have a set of twin nieces a few years older than you. They're identical, just like you, but I can tell them apart."

The next few minutes were spent in a whirlwind of questions about Walker's nieces, then buckling the girls in the back seat of Hope's rental. He straightened, caught her eye over the top of the car. "I'll meet you at the store." He rattled off the address. "Twenty minutes, tops."

"We'll be there."

Hands stuffed in his pockets, Walker watched Hope drive out of the parking lot and then turn in the direction of Main Street.

As he made his way back inside the hospital, he mentally reviewed the events of the morning. It didn't take him long to come to the conclusion that Hope Jeffries hadn't been completely honest with him. She claimed she'd come to Thunder Ridge simply to introduce her nieces to their father.

That wasn't the only reason. She wanted something else. He had a few ideas what that was, and none of them boded well for Brent or the rest of the family.

But he was getting ahead of himself. Best to let

the woman think she had the upper hand. In the meantime, Walker would get to know his nieces better. His throat caught on a breath and all he could think was that those sweet little girls were his nieces. Family. His family.

No way to predict how Brent would react to the news that he was a father of twins. But now that Walker had met Harper and Kennedy, he wasn't going to let them go without a fight. A plan began forming in his brain.

First step: gather more information.

After changing out of his scrubs, Walker grabbed the rest of his gear and a few necessary items for building a spectacular snowman. He arrived outside Quinn's shop with five minutes to spare. He cut the engine of his SUV and ran through what he knew about the twins, their mother and their aunt.

Not very much.

Walker didn't even know where Hope and the girls lived, or what Hope did for a living. He figured some sort of fancy, designer job. The woman had city written all over her. She was also successful, or at least comfortable enough to purchase fancy coats for herself and the twins.

Money wasn't her motivation. Unless she'd spent her last dime on those coats, and...

He was speculating.

No decision needed to be made until he spoke

with Brent, which could prove more problematic than he'd let on. Walker pulled out his phone, checked for incoming texts. Nothing. He wasn't surprised.

Walker had been telling the truth when he told Hope that communication between the brothers was difficult. Sometimes it was due to technology. Brent chose to work in some of the remotest regions in Africa. But there was another reason, mostly Walker's fault.

Calculating the time difference, he sent another text. This one briefer than the last, only two words. Call me.

No response.

Walker opened his contacts next, scrolled to the *Q*s, then pressed on his sister's name. Quinn answered on the second ring. "What do you want?"

"Is that how you greet your favorite brother?"

"At the moment, you are most definitely not my favorite brother."

"*Good morning, Walker.* How hard is that?"

"Fine. *Good morning, Walker.*" She still sounded distracted, and he could hear the sound of machines coupled with incomprehensible chatter in the background. "Now, what do you want? I'm elbow-deep in melting chocolate."

"Pull yourself away and let me in the shop."

"And why would I do that?"

"I promised hot chocolate to a woman and two

very sweet little girls." Walker climbed out of his car, then shouldered the door shut behind him. "Help me out, okay?"

"I…wait. Are you on a date?"

His stomach dipped. "It's not a date."

Silence met the statement.

Quinn's shock wasn't unexpected. It was no secret that Walker hadn't even looked at another woman, much less gone on a date since Rachel's death. He'd blamed work, but those who knew him best suspected he was using that as an excuse to hide from the world. They were correct. "Open the shop, Quinn. It's important."

"All right, all right. But this better be good."

He thought of Hope and the twins. "It is."

The next words out of Quinn's mouth were, "Alexa, disconnect."

The line went dead.

"Goodbye to you, too, sis." Shaking his head, Walker stuffed his phone into his back pocket and stepped onto the sidewalk. He caught sight of Hope and the twins hurrying toward him.

Well, Harper and Kennedy hurried. Hope moved at a more sedate pace.

When the twins saw him, they broke out in a run. Walker was working on zero hours of sleep, but the sight of those girls rushing to meet him energized him as no cup of coffee could.

He crouched, automatically opening his arms

as if he'd been greeting them this way since they could toddle. Without an ounce of hesitation, Harper and Kennedy rushed into his embrace. The scent of baby shampoo filled his nose.

He set the girls at arm's length and smiled.

They grinned back. This easy familiarity outside the hospital wasn't typical for him, and he sensed it wasn't for them either. The sadness in them recognized the sadness in him. Loss had a way of drawing grief-stricken souls to each other. Walker had spent years pushing people away and keeping his distance from personal connections. For some reason he didn't feel the need to do either with these children.

Had the Lord brought the twins into Walker's life for a reason?

Hope came up behind the twins. She stopped in the middle of a single ray of sunlight. Her hair took on a golden glow, giving her an ethereal look. Her moss green eyes were radiant and full of an emotion Walker couldn't define. Love for the girls, but also concern, or maybe that was trepidation? She hadn't seemed afraid before. Angry, wary, a little hostile, but not afraid.

Was she worried Brent would take the girls away from her? Walker took a harder look at Hope Jeffries. She'd taken a risk coming here. Why?

That was the million-dollar question. For all he

knew, she was gathering information about Brent and his family to use against them in a custody battle. She wouldn't win. Brent was their father. She was only their aunt. A DNA test would settle the matter.

But he was getting ahead of himself again. Hope could do the right thing. She could also make a lot of trouble for Brent.

Not on Walker's watch. "Thanks for coming," he said.

"I always keep my promises."

Good to know.

She ran her gaze over him. "You changed clothes."

"Scrubs aren't the best choice for rolling around in the snow."

"I suppose not." Something came and went in her eyes before she switched her attention to the building behind him, her eyes narrowing. "The shop looks closed."

"Quinn is in the back." He looked over his shoulder and saw his sister making her way through the darkened store. "Here she comes now."

While they waited for Walker's sister, Hope took a closer look at her surroundings, taking note of the nearby businesses. Most had charming, almost whimsical names. The Wash and

Spins, a sort of laundromat and dance studio hybrid; The Slippery Slope, a ski shop that could use a bit more Christmas decorations; a restaurant called Señor O'Malley's. What an odd name. She tried to imagine what sort of food they served.

She returned her gaze to Quinn's Sweet Shop. The type of business was self-explanatory.

Any minute now, the twins would meet Walker's sister, who was their aunt and yet another person who could take them away from Hope.

She watched as a slim silhouette worked the locks of the shop's glass door. The form was covered in flickering shadows, making it difficult for Hope to make out the woman's features. But when the door swung open and the store owner stepped into the light, one glance told Hope this was Walker's sister Quinn.

She had the same dark hair and blue, blue eyes as her brother and the twins. It wasn't just the color, but the shape, as well. The features were similar, as were the full lips. That was some strong DNA, Hope thought. A test would be superfluous. She would ask for one anyway.

Walker made the introductions. "Quinn, this is Hope Jeffries."

"Pleased to meet you, Hope Jeffries."

"Likewise."

The apron that covered Quinn's black wool pants and pale pink sweater had streaks of flour and what looked like melted chocolate. A big, shiny diamond ring hung from a sturdy-looking chain around her neck. The smile she gave Hope was reminiscent of her brother's. She directed that welcoming grin onto the girls, winning points with Hope for speaking to them directly. "And who might you be?"

"I'm Kennedy. And this is my twin sister, Harper. We're five."

Quinn's smile widened. "What a great age. I have twin girls. They're a little older than you, almost seven." She angled her head. "I adore your hats."

"Aunt Hope bought them for us."

"Your aunt has excellent taste." She aimed a wink in Hope's direction.

Kennedy tugged on Quinn's apron. "You look like Dr. Walker."

Quinn eyed her brother, her gaze serious. "That's because I'm Dr. Walker's older, wiser sister." She continued looking at him then shifted her gaze to Hope, her eyes slightly narrowed. "What do you say we get out of this cold and you can tell me how you know my brother?"

"We just met him this morning."

"Is that so?" She held his gaze. "I smell a story."

"You'll get it," Walker promised, not quite meeting his sister's eyes. "Right now, the twins want hot chocolate, and everyone knows you make the best in town."

"This is true." She offered a hand to Harper, then the other to Kennedy. "Come with me."

They reached out to her without question and let her guide them into the store.

Walker waved Hope inside ahead of him. She started forward, navigated the first step, then swung back around. With him still at street level, they were nearly eye to eye. She could see the different shades of blue in his eyes and the lines of fatigue at the edges. The grooves were deep, as if he'd been operating without sufficient sleep for a very long time.

Some strange instinct nearly had her lifting her hand to smooth away that mix of sadness and bafflement in his eyes. Hope resisted, barely. She understood his confusion, even sympathized. She'd had months to process the reality of her sister's quick wedding, and all that came after. Walker had only found out less than an hour ago.

"The twins don't know why we're in town," she told him. "I'd like it to stay that way, at least until I have a chance to speak with their father."

"Hope. We're on the same side."

"What side is that?"

"The twins'."

She sighed. "I've insulted you. That wasn't my

intent. I just wanted to make sure you understood the fragile nature of the situation."

"Look. I know this is a big ask. But you're going to have to trust me." Frustration sounded in his voice, and showed in the way he pressed his thumb and forefinger to the bridge of his nose. "Can you do that?"

"I…" She paused, then nodded slowly. "Yes. I can." *For now.*

"Thank you."

A moment of solidarity passed between them.

Before she did something crazy, like reach out to him, she spun around and stepped into the pleasant scent of chocolate and sugar.

Quinn had stopped in the middle of the shop. Hands on her knees, she was currently leaning down and addressing the twins directly. "Now that I know your names, tell me, who wants hot chocolate?"

Two little hands shot in the air.

"Me, too." Quinn walked to one of the walls and pressed several buttons. Soon the interior of the store was bathed in a soft, golden glow. The twins gasped in delight.

Hope did the same. The decor was decidedly French, with pink and brown the dominating colors. Shelves loaded with a variety of gift baskets lined the wall behind a waist-high counter. The display cases were filled with every kind of confection any self-respecting sweet lover could ever want. "I adore your shop."

Smiling, Quinn moved to an industrial-looking machine and started working a series of knobs and switches. "It's a labor of love."

"I can tell." Hope spun in a circle, not sure what called to her most. The baskets of chocolate, the colorful macarons or the chocolate-covered popcorn. Her mouth watered. "The girls and I thought about stopping in here yesterday, but we wanted cupcakes, so we went to the bakery down the street instead."

"I'm sorry to hear that." Quinn's voice held zero judgment, but the stiffness in her shoulders indicated disappointment. "I make cupcakes, too."

"So I see." Hope moved closer to the display case and studied the selections. "Are those as good as they look?"

"Better." Walker drew alongside her.

"You know, Harper and Kennedy—" Quinn reached for an empty mug as she spoke "—you girls look a lot like my daughters."

"Do they like to make snowmen?" Harper wanted to know.

"Absolutely. We take our snowmen very seriously in this family." An unspoken question was in the look she shot Walker. "Maybe my brother will bring you over to my house this weekend and you can see what I mean."

"Can we, Aunt Hope?"

"We'll see."

Before either could object, Quinn was directing the twins toward a darling, kid-size table. She set a steaming mug in front of each girl. "Blow on it, it's hot."

Harper did as she requested. Kennedy, however, was too busy frowning in her mug to obey. "She has more marshmallows than I do."

"No, she doesn't," Quinn corrected in the gentle manner of a mother used to little girls arguing over marshmallows. "You each have seven."

Kennedy counted—out loud—only relenting once she discovered she had the promised seven.

"Here." Quinn handed Walker a mug. "You're officially on duty. Watch the girls while Hope and I have a little chat in the back."

Walker bounced his gaze between Hope and his sister. "I don't think that's a good idea."

"It's okay," Hope told him. "Really."

"Be right back." Quinn linked arms with Hope and drew her through a set of swinging double doors that led into the shop's massive kitchen. A team of employees hovered over workstations. Not a single person glanced in their direction. Complicated looking machines whirred, while giant mixers churned at a slow and steady pace.

All in all, a successful business in motion. A very loud successful business. Hope could hardly hear herself think.

Quinn took up a position near a large plate glass window, her back to the shop, which allowed Hope a direct line of sight to where Walker sat at the small table with the twins. The man should look ridiculous in that tiny little chair with his knees up to his chin. He looked perfectly at home, as if he'd had tea parties—or rather, hot chocolate parties—on a regular basis. Something like affection swept through her. "He's good with them."

Quinn glanced over her shoulder, sighed softly. There was sadness in the sound. When she turned around there was also the look of a protective big sister in her stance, something Hope would never have a chance to practice on Charity's behalf. Now she was sad.

"Walker has always had a knack with kids." Quinn's eyes never left Hope's face. "Even before he marri—" she cleared her throat "—before he became an ER doctor."

Hope had questions. Unfortunately, Quinn had questions, as well, and didn't waste time voicing them. "What's going on between you and Walker?"

"It's complicated."

"Most things are when a woman shows up

with two little girls that look like my brother, and every bit like my own daughters, save for a slight difference in hair color. So, I'm going to ask again, what's going on between you and Walker?"

Hope shifted from one foot to the other. She hadn't expected an interrogation. The Evans were proving kind, but also formidable. If they closed ranks on her…no. She wasn't going to go there just yet. "Your brother and I only met this morning."

All signs of patience disappeared, replaced with a slight stiffening of shoulders. The worried expression was back, as well. "I see."

"I don't think you do."

"I heard the girls call you Aunt Hope. Where's their mother?"

"Dead." The word came out hard and a little cold, a perfect companion to the emotion spreading through her heart. She'd lost all sense of polite behavior. Hope hadn't come to Thunder Ridge to be thrown on the defensive. She'd come because Charity could not.

As if understanding her pain, Quinn's expression softened. "I'm sorry for your loss."

Thrown off guard, again, she forced out a response through tight lips. "Thank you."

"I'm going to speak plainly, and I ask that you do the same."

Hope nodded.

"Is Walker…" Quinn let her words trail off, spun around, frowned at the sight of her brother laughing over something one of the twins just said. "I can't believe I'm asking you this, because it seems so out of character, and the timing is pretty close to impossible, but is Walker the father of those girls out there?"

"No."

Quinn's relief was palpable.

"Your brother Brent is their father."

"Walker Bartholomew Evans. A word, if you please. Now."

Walker met his sister's eyes. The look she leveled on him supplied all the information he needed. Quinn knew about Brent and the twins.

Setting down his mug, he told the girls, "Be right back," and then stood.

He passed Hope halfway across the shop. In that moment, when their eyes met and held, he knew. He knew, as sure as he knew his own name, that Hope Jeffries had come to Thunder Ridge with a plan firmly in place, one that would put them on opposite sides of a fight.

A shame, he thought. He possibly could have grown to like her. The thought felt like a betrayal to the woman he'd promised to love until death do us part.

"You told Quinn about Brent, your sister and the twins."

"She knows enough."

"How did she take the news?"

"About the same as you, with equal amounts of shock and a weird sort of acceptance." She eyed him thoughtfully. "Why is that? What aren't you telling me about your brother?"

"No idea what you mean," Walker hedged. No good would come from sharing too much information.

After shooting her a final glance, he joined his sister in the kitchen, then motioned her to follow him to her private office where they couldn't be overheard. An unnecessary precaution due to the high volume of noise, but Walker wasn't taking any chances. Brent deserved a chance to do the right thing before the gossip started.

Walker waited for Quinn to enter the room, then shut the door behind him.

"So," Quinn began. "Are we absolutely sure Brent is the father?"

"Pretty much." He rattled off the wedding date, followed up with the girls' birthday approximately nine months later. "He'll need to take a DNA test, but that'll prove more a formality. Hope has proof. I've seen it."

"Okay, okay." She blew out a breath. "Okay."

"This is a good thing, Quinn. The twins are amazing."

"Yeah, yeah, I know, of course. You're right. I just need a moment to process all of this." Drawing in a deep breath, she rubbed the back of her neck. "How long have you known?"

"For about—" he checked the time on his watch "—an hour and a half."

His answer seemed to shock her. "I'm confused. Why did Hope contact you?"

"It's complicated."

"Hmm." Quinn eyed him closely. "You're hiding something."

Walker quickly filled her in on what he knew. Which was, admittedly, not much. "I'll get the rest out of Hope this morning."

Quinn didn't seem to hear him. She was too busy tapping her fingertip on her chin and looking off into the distance. "We need to call a family meeting."

"Agreed." The siblings congregated at Quinn's every Sunday afternoon following church. But Sunday was too many days away.

"I'll set it up for later tonight. Say, seven." Quinn pulled her cell phone from a pocket in her apron. "Will you be able to attend?" she asked without looking up from the screen.

"I'm off the next two nights."

"Excellent."

While she typed, Walker added, "I've reached out to Brent, twice. He hasn't replied."

"Not surprised."

Walker wasn't either. Regret was an uncomfortable emotion.

"I'll reach out, too." Quinn's fingers slowed. "Okay, done."

A second later, a ding indicated Walker had a new group text. He pulled out his phone, read the message. Typical Quinn. She'd been cryptic, but insistent. Emergency family meeting, 7:00 p.m., my house. No excuses except broken bones or death.

Responses came in at a rapid pace, ranging from I'll be there to What's up? To Casey's Are you kidding me right now? I have a hot date tonight!

Quinn answered: I said NO EXCUSES unless you are broken or dead. You will be both if you don't show up.

Walker snorted. "Way to tap into your softer side."

"That was my softer side." Grinning, she stuffed her phone into the back pocket of her jeans. "You should bring Hope and the twins. The girls can play with Sinclair and Skylar while we discuss next steps."

"That's the plan." When Walker returned to the main area of the shop, the girls were finished drinking their hot chocolate. "Ready to build a snowman?"

Kennedy clapped her hands. "Can he be as tall as you?"

"We might want to start with something a little more manageable."

"Okay, if you say so."

Walker grinned. Apparently, hot chocolate made little girls agreeable. Women too, because Hope dutifully followed them out of the shop without a single argument.

The twins launched into a popular children's song about building snowmen. Their voices rang with pure joy, if a bit off-key. Their enthusiasm was infectious, the kind of ease that came from childhood innocence and the resiliency of youth.

Walker couldn't deny wanting a little of that innocence, knowing he'd never be able to capture what he'd lost. Scripture spoke of having the faith of a child. Faith. Trust that the Lord was in control. Walker had once carried that in his heart. He'd cut himself off from personal relationships beyond family for so long he'd nearly forgotten how to feel much of anything beyond getting from one minute to the next.

Harper skipped beside him. Taking his hand, she asked, "Are we there yet?"

"Almost." He spoke to Hope over the child's head. "Quinn called a family meeting for tonight.

She wants to tell the rest of our siblings about…
you know. I'd like you to be there."

She nodded.

"The twins can play with Quinn's daughters
while we all talk."

"Oh, I—" she went silent a moment "—I suppose that will be all right."

"Come on," Kennedy urged. "You're going too
slow."

Seeing their destination at last, the twins
rushed into the park, singing and laughing and
kicking up snow.

Walker attempted to pick up his pace, but Hope
stopped him with a touch to his arm. "I'm not
sure the girls have ever made a snowman before."
She glanced toward them, worry creasing across
her brow. "I don't know why they lied."

"They wanted to impress an adult. It's common
with children their age, especially after suffering
a traumatic loss."

"How do you know that?"

"My job is to diagnose. I can't do that if I don't
listen to what patients tell me, and what they
leave out." The girls called his name. He called
back, "On my way."

Trotting over, he knelt beside them, then
scooped up a handful of snow, packing, testing,
rolling it around in his palms.

Kennedy leaned over his arm. "What are you doing?"

"Seeing what kind of snow we have to work with. Good news—" he rolled the ball around in his hand "—it's perfect."

He added more snow, kept packing until the tiny clump was perfectly round.

With the twins mimicking him, Walker kept adding snow to his. By the time the mound was too big to hold, the girls had given up on their attempts and were watching him with wide eyes.

"All right." He set the snowball on the ground. "Let's roll."

Chapter Five

Hope hung back, torn between joining the fun and simply watching Walker and the twins. The snowball that had once fit in his gloved palm quickly grew to the size of a large boulder.

Apparently, the man did know what he was doing.

The atmosphere among the trio was full of cheer, joyful even. Hope hadn't seen the twins this happy in months, maybe ever. She felt a slight relaxing of her body. Drawing in a slow, careful breath, she let the scent of pine trees and freshly fallen snow fill her nose.

Standing here, in what she guessed was the beating heart of Thunder Ridge, was like being wrapped in a festive Christmas present. Bows, garland, wreaths and ribbon dominated every available space. The gazebo nestled on the edge of the park also had tiny fairy lights and silver bells.

She spun in a circle, taking it all in, falling in love with the scene, the town. She slammed her eyes shut against the longing that spread through her. Christmas, family, how she missed them. But that made no sense. How could she miss something she never really had?

Opening her eyes, she shouted over the girls' laughter. "That is going to be one big snowman."

Walker gave her a pointed look. "You going to get over here and help?"

Hope took a step in his direction, paused. It wasn't that she didn't want to join the fun. It was that she didn't know how. She'd spent her life watching from the sidelines, alone and unnoticed. She was a thinker. Losing herself in her head had become comfortable, normal, safe, a barrier between her and the unknown world.

"You know—" Walker made a grand show of struggling under the weight of the now insanely large snowball "—this would go smoother with an extra pair of hands."

"On my way."

She tugged on her gloves and took a step. But when she heard a dog barking, she stopped cold.

An enormous, absolutely gorgeous Saint Bernard came into view. The excited animal danced at the feet of his owner, a tall man dressed in dark-washed jeans and a blue ski jacket. A camera with a large lens hung from his neck. He moved with long, languid strides, the pace slow and lazy, as if he had nowhere special to be. Hope thought she recognized him but needed a closer look to be certain.

Walker paused mid-roll, and then pointed to the newcomers. "Stop right there."

Man and dog ignored him.

"I mean it." Walker glared at the other man. "Control your beast."

Said beast performed a high-kick dance in place, its face full of goofy dog joy.

"My girl is harmless as they come, aren't you, baby?" The man kissed the dog's head, then aimed a narrow-eyed glance at the emerging snowman. "And you're doing that all wrong. I taught you better. Put your shoulders into it."

"Stay back, McCoy." Walker lifted his palm in the air. "Leave this to the experts."

"Since you asked so nicely." The dog owner— McCoy—let the excited animal off her leash.

She did two fast spins, impressive considering her size, and then sped across the park, clumps of snow flying in her wake. Walker intercepted the animal before she got near the twins. The dog greeted him with a doggy dance and loud, happy barks.

"There she is. There's my sweet girl." Walker reached down and framed the dog's face in his hands. "When you gonna leave your mean owner and come live with me?"

The Saint Bernard barked at him.

"I know we'll be very happy together." He kissed the animal on the snout.

Not to be outdone, the dog reared up on her hind legs, planted her large paws on his shoulders and slurped her big pink tongue across his face.

He laughed. "Yuck."

She repeated the public display of affection.

"Yeah, yeah, I love you, too. Now get off me, you big doofus." He calmed the dog down with soft, soothing words and gentle strokes. "Come meet my friends."

Hope had a moment of sheer terror when he started guiding the dog toward the twins. But the dog followed Walker at a slow, sedate pace, behaving more like a pampered house cat than a dog the size of a small horse.

Walker told the animal to drop. She immediately did as commanded, grinning up at him as if he were her long lost love.

Walker motioned the twins closer. They were clearly nervous, but also filled with anticipation. Hope knew the feeling. She'd always wanted a dog, the bigger and sloppier the better. It hadn't been possible. A dog required a yard, which came with a house, which meant her father would have had to stay in the States and care for his daughters.

He'd chosen mission work abroad over his family.

That memory had no place here. So, Hope focused on watching Walker show the twins how to pet the dog. "You want to follow the direction her fur grows. Like this. Yes, perfect, that's it. Good girl, Bertha," he praised the dog for sitting still. "Try again, Harper. Excellent. Now you, Kennedy."

Caught up in the sweet moment, Hope laid a hand on her heart. She drew in a tight breath, and then sighed it back out. Thoughts of "what if" ran through her mind.

Captured by the possibility, she forgot that Bertha came with an owner. "Hey," he said, approaching her.

Hope started. "Oh, sorry. I…" She concentrated on calming her breath. "Hello. I didn't see you standing there."

"I can be stealthy." The smile he gave her brought back the image of the Evans siblings in the silver picture frame.

"You're Walker's brother. The…artist?"

"Sculptor, actually. And photographer." He pointed to the camera slung around his neck.

"I remember now. Your name is McCoy."

"That's me."

Three Evans siblings down, two to go. No, make that three if she counted Brent.

"And now I'm feeling as if I missed the opening of a Broncos game and we're deep in the second quarter. You are...?"

"I'm Hope. Hope Jeffries."

"Well, Hope. Hope Jeffries. Pleased to meet you."

He stuck out his hand, a slightly flirty smile on his lips. He had the Evanses' stunning good looks, but unlike when Walker looked at her like that, she felt nothing. No hitch in her breathing. No ping in her heart.

Realizing he was waiting for her to take his hand, she pressed her palm against his, and again, no spark, no visceral response like the first time she'd touched Walker's hand. Or every other time they connected physically. A brush of fingers, a touch to her arm.

She pulled free of McCoy's grip.

He shifted his stance slightly and glanced over at the scene playing out with Walker, Bertha and the twins. After a moment, he turned back and zeroed in on Hope's face. "You're a friend of Walker's?"

"Not really," she admitted, then gave him what was becoming her standard line. "We just met this morning."

"He seems pretty friendly with your...daughters?" He asked the question in the same tentative way she'd asked about his profession.

She answered him with equal brevity. "Nieces."

"Ah."

Silence fell over them. She tried not to fidget or fill the awkward moment with words. Just as well. McCoy's attention remained glued to his brother and the twins.

He angled his head, contemplated the scene another moment, then turned back to Hope. "You know, when I first entered the park, I thought Walker was playing with my nieces."

"I—I'm sorry, did you call Harper and Kennedy your nieces?"

How did he know? Wow, Quinn worked fast. She must have contacted her siblings as soon as Hope left her office.

"I'm not talking about *your* nieces. But mine. Sinclair and Skylar are bigger than your girls, probably because they're older. Maybe. I don't know much about kids, which could explain why I think they all look alike." He laughed, sobered a second later, narrowed his eyes. "Maybe…"

Hope opened her mouth, shut it. She didn't know how to respond to McCoy's obvious confusion. Of course the two sets of twins looked alike. They were cousins. That wasn't something she could just blurt out. Or could she?

McCoy didn't seem to notice her silent battle. "Speaking of Quinn, that reminds me, she sent me a text this morning. I ignored it." He shrugged. "She's always sending texts. We call her the social chairman of the family."

Hope laughed.

"Excuse me a minute." He pulled out his phone, thumbed it to life and then studied the screen. "Huh."

He tapped a quick reply, then returned the phone to his back pocket. His eyebrows slammed together. "Would you look at that, Walker is actually smiling."

Hope followed the direction of his gaze. Walker was, indeed, smiling. Why would that be such a shock?

With a quick, effortless move, McCoy whipped the camera up to his face. A series of clicks followed, then several more. Hope studied the scene, wondering what he was capturing.

And then she knew. Walker and the twins.

Her heart pinged. This wasn't the first time she'd felt the sensation. She didn't like it any more now than she had the first time.

Walker had dropped to his knees, laughing. Kennedy clung to his back like a koala bear. Harper was on the ground still petting Bertha with slow, careful strokes.

The three of them looked like a family, a happy, functional, normal family. And McCoy Evans was capturing the moment with his camera.

He continued clicking away, completely unaware of how Hope was reacting. She could feel the twins slipping away with each shutter of the camera.

What have I done? She should have never brought Harper and Kennedy to Thunder Ridge with her. She should have made the trip alone.

Too late.

No. No, it wasn't. Brent could deny they were his daughters. Hope could still win custody.

But would Walker and his siblings happily hand them over to her without a fight? Possibly, maybe...but not likely.

By the time McCoy lowered the camera, she was in a full panic.

"As much as I've enjoyed meeting you, I have an appointment in—" he glanced at the chunky black watch on his wrist "—five minutes ago. Sorry, gotta go."

McCoy whistled one long shrill note through his fingertips. Bertha hopped to her feet, swung away from Harper without actually touching the child, then trotted over to her master.

"Good girl." McCoy clicked the leash to the dog's harness and said to Hope, "See you around."

She watched man and dog saunter away.

She glanced back at Walker, allowing herself one, long look into his piercing blue eyes, then felt her own narrow. The man was working a sizeable handful of snow into a tidy little ball.

"You better put that snowball down," Hope warned, hands on hips.

His grin flashed, quick and devastating. "Are you questioning my motives, Ms. Jeffries?"

She looked frantically around for shelter. She found and discarded several options. Then. There. Perfect. Inching toward the bushy pine tree, she picked up speed when Walker mimicked the windup of a professional baseball pitcher.

The snowball sailed through the air in a wide, looping arc. And…smack!

"Hey!" She brushed the snow off her right shoulder. "You, Dr. Evans, just crossed a line."

He rubbed his hands together. "Now we're talking."

Walker couldn't remember having this much fun in years.

He didn't let his mind go any further than that. Instead, he concentrated on watching Hope's retreat behind a snow-covered pine tree.

"You can run, Hope Jeffries, but you can't hide."

She spewed out a muffled threat that included a bunch of nonsense and a reference to a former softball career in high school.

Laughing, he formed his next frosty weapon with the quick, sure hands of a man who'd won his share of snowball fights. Unbeknownst to his opponent, Walker had the patience of a younger brother in a large family bent on teaching him the pecking order. His siblings had underestimated him. And so, too, had Hope. When Walker Evans set his mind on something, he had the tenacity of a bulldog with a meaty bone.

"You gonna come out anytime this year?"

She made the mistake of peaking around the tree. He fired. And missed.

"You have no idea who you're up against." Since she made the ridiculous threat from behind a tree large enough to hide a small SUV, Walker took his time reloading.

A mistake in judgment. Hope pelted him in the chest with three snowballs. "Impressive aim," he called out.

"I told you I pitched for my high school softball team."

Okay, then.

The twins realized they were missing out on the fun. Walker immediately claimed them for his team. "You make the snowballs," he suggested. "I'll throw them."

Proving to be excellent recruits, the girls got to straight work.

"Hey," Hope called out from behind the tree. "That's three against one."

"Yeah, yeah, a tiny little insignificant detail."

Nevertheless, in the spirit of fair play, Walker switched jobs with the girls.

Playing along, Hope came out from behind the tree to give then an easier target. Harper and Kennedy attacked, mostly missing, but Walker praised them for their effort. As did Hope.

She came closer, closer, tossing a snowball from one hand to the other. The twins screeched, running for shelter behind Walker. He opened his mouth to call a truce, but Hope was having none of it. Smiling sweetly, she lifted onto her toes, came eye to eye with him, then smashed the snowball in his face.

He blinked in surprise. Torn between laughing and taking revenge, he settled on roping his arms around her waist and pulling her against him.

"What are you doing?"

Blinking snow out of his eyes, he gave the twins a sidelong glance. "Who wants to learn how to make a snow angel?"

"Me!" they screamed in unison.

"You're in luck. Your aunt has agreed to demonstrate the proper technique." Hooking his foot around the back of her knees, he dumped her gently atop the snow-covered ground.

Flat on her back, she glared. "You are not a nice man."

"Many people in town would disagree."

The twins leaned over her. Harper spoke for

the duo. "She's not moving." She swung her gaze up to Walker. "Is she supposed to just lay there like that?"

"She's supposed to move her arms and legs, up and down, in and out, kind of like horizontal jumping jacks."

"I know how to make a snow angel." Hope growled at him. She actually growled. The woman made him smile. It had been a long time since Walker had smiled so much.

"We're waiting."

"Fine." Lips pressed tightly together, she went through the motions, finishing up by pressing her head back into the snow.

"Well done," he praised, earning him another growl.

Laughing, he reached out and waited for Hope to accept his assistance.

Slowly, clearly reluctant, she placed her hands in his. He yanked her up, catching her against him before her feet touched the ground.

The past melted away and his mind went blank but for the woman in his arms. He drew in a sharp breath, his heart beating wildly in his chest.

"My turn," Kennedy declared, the interruption restoring his equilibrium.

A little mournfully, Walker set Hope on the ground, then turned to the bouncing child beside him. "Let's find a clean spot in the snow."

He picked up Kennedy, dumped her gently in the snow and said, "Don't move." Then he repeated the process with her sister. "Okay, go!"

They went a little crazy, but got the job done. In silent agreement, he and Hope pulled the girls to their feet. Kennedy spun around and grinned at him. "That was fun."

Her eyes shone from beneath her dark winged eyebrows, another undeniable Evans trait. Was this what his child would have looked like, Walker wondered? Would she have been this pretty, this sweet and innocent? His knees buckled under the onslaught of emotion that washed over him. Some old and familiar, others fresh and almost optimistic.

It was as if a switch had been flipped in his mind. He hovered in a moment between past and present. His limbs suddenly felt heavy, the kind of weight that came after a long slumber.

"Can we finish the snowman now?"

He had to look away before answering. He swallowed, twice, then managed to say, "Let's do this."

Eyes burning, he took off toward the half-finished snowman. The twins trotted alongside him. Although she moved at a slower pace, Hope followed along, too.

Walker watched her out of the corner of his eye. He couldn't stop thinking about her in his arms. They'd fit nicely together, pretty close to perfectly, her head the exact height for him to rest his chin at the crown. His hands itched to pull her close again, to see if she still smelled of lavender and the great outdoors.

Needing a moment to calm his pulse, he smoothed his hand over the snowman's lower body. For the next ten minutes, Walker focused on the mechanics of stacking three snowballs on top of one another, largest to smallest, while Hope and the twins packed snow between the gaps.

"Nicely done," he said, stepping back to eye the finished product.

Kennedy wasn't even a little impressed. "He doesn't look right."

"That's because he's not finished yet. Hang tight." Walker retrieved the gym bag he'd brought alone. He pulled out a baseball cap, a blue bandana and a few other items he'd gathered from the hospital's break room.

The twins brought the snowman to life.

"Best snowman ever," Hope declared.

"He does have something special," Walker agreed.

The twins launched into an impromptu happy dance that was about as graceful as Bertha's had been earlier, and just as infectious. Walker watched with his heart in his throat. *Brent has lost so much time with them.*

He vowed to redouble his efforts to get in touch with his brother.

Hope met Walker's gaze over the twirling, spinning girls. Something came into her smile. Gratitude. Relief. Fear. And then, determination. A woman preparing for a fight.

"We've monopolized your morning long enough," she said, her voice full of apology and something else, something that put distance between them. He would know. It was a tactic he used often enough.

"I'm good." Granted, he was running on adrenaline at this point, but he wasn't sorry for it. He could sleep next week.

"You're exhausted. Let's go, girls. We need to let Dr. Evans get on with his day."

The arguments began at once.

The twins' reluctance to leave his company gave Walker a kick in the gut. As did Hope's use of his formal title. He wasn't Dr. Evans. He was Uncle Walker.

Now wasn't the time to make that distinction. But soon.

"You'll see Dr. Evans later tonight. Say goodbye."

"Please, call me Dr. Walker," he told the girls, which earned him two identical grins and would make the transition to Uncle Walker much easier.

"But we don't want to say goodbye, Dr. Walker," Harper whined. "We're still having fun."

Me, too, Walker thought, only half shocked at this point by the revelation. He'd flown solo for years and been just fine with that. Or at least resolute. In a matter of hours, the twins had broken through his defenses. He wasn't sorry for it.

No matter what Brent had done to their mother, or what she'd done to him, the twins were family. Harper and Kennedy deserved to know their aunts and uncles and cousins. They also deserved to know their father.

Hope had custody of the girls, for now. Could she make a case against Brent? Without more information, Walker simply didn't know.

He needed to speak with Brent.

If his brother didn't want to be a part of his daughters' lives—and that was a big if—Walker would work with Hope to formulate a plan for the future.

Would she play nice?

Something cold moved through him, wrapping around his heart, redoubling his resolve. If Hope Jeffries had come for a fight, she would get one. "I need your contact information."

She flinched at his abrupt tone. "You think I'm going to run."

He said nothing.

"I came all this way. I'm not going to run now."

Still saying nothing, he held her gaze.

"Fine." She pushed out a sharp breath. "Give me your phone."

He tugged his cell out of his back pocket. She sent herself a quick text from his phone so he would have her information.

Walker studied the screen before tucking the phone back into his pocket and saying, "I don't recognize your area code."

She lifted a shoulder. "The girls and I live on the East Coast."

Though not unexpected, her vague response put him on guard. She'd come halfway across the country to introduce the girls to their father out of the goodness of her heart? No, there was more to it. Either she would tell him, or Walker would find out on his own. "Where are you staying in town?"

"At the Grand Palace Hotel on Main Street."

"The meeting at Quinn's is set for seven o'clock tonight. I'll pick you all up at six thirty."

"I'll drive us to your sister's house."

Walker started to argue, then thought better of it. He couldn't ask Hope to trust him, if he didn't do the same.

"Suit yourself." He gave her Quinn's address, then placed his hands on his knees. "See you later, girls."

They jumped into his arms. As he held them

close, his heart swelled with love—so fast, so unexpected. He pulled in a hard breath. There was a ragged quality to the sound that made him shut his eyes. The moment passed, and he let them wiggle free.

Hope said her own goodbye with a little too much enthusiasm. Which wasn't suspicious at all.

Once she and the twins were out of earshot, Walker retrieved his cell phone again. He called his attorney's private number. Mitchell St. James, a friend since middle school, answered with a smile in his voice. "Hey, Walker, what's up?"

"We need to talk, Mitch."

A pause. Then, "You got a legal problem?"

"Maybe, yeah. I think I do."

"Too bad." A rustle of papers filled the next few seconds. "I have an opening tomorrow at two thirty."

Tomorrow. Walker experienced a slight dropping sensation in his stomach. Although he'd rather meet with Mitch today, he knew the attorney was a busy man. Which meant he probably had to switch a few things around to fit Walker in so quickly.

"That works," he said into the phone. "See you then."

Chapter Six

Back at the hotel, Hope helped the girls out of their coats. Kennedy yawned. Harper copied her. Despite their exhaustion, neither twin could stop talking about their "new friend" Dr. Walker, or the big dog with the super soft fur.

"Yes," Hope agreed with her heart in her throat. "Bertha was very pretty."

"Can we get a dog just like her?" Kennedy asked around another yawn.

Hope murmured a noncommittal answer, then suggested, "What do you say we take a nap?"

Half-hearted arguments followed, accompanied with another round of yawns that proved just how tired they were.

"That settles it." A smile tugged at Hope's lips as she tucked them in the queen-size bed the two had shared the night before.

Covers up to her chin, Kennedy looked up at

Hope with an expectant, wide-eyed expression. "When will we see Dr. Walker again?"

Hope answered the question as she had every other time the child had asked. "Later tonight."

"Good." Another yawn. "I like him."

Hope tried not to sigh. Of course the child liked Walker. He'd been spontaneous and easy with the girls, something that had never come naturally to Hope. It wasn't that she didn't try. She simply didn't know how. Even as a child, she'd been more reserved than other kids, which had carried over into adulthood.

From the moment Charity had arrived on her doorstep, Hope had been out of her element with the twins. Dr. Stephens had suggested she let the relationship grow organically. But Hope wasn't one to sit around and wait. She'd read every article and book about child development she could find. She'd attended workshops, asked advice from day care workers and had sought out experts at her university.

She'd also prayed. A lot. She'd searched the Bible for direction, as well. She found the most concrete advice in Proverbs, especially Proverbs 22, which said *Train up a child in the way he should go: and when he is old, he will not depart from it.*

With that in mind, Hope had taken the twins to church every Sunday. Yet here she was, months after assuming sole custody and she was still searching for that relaxed sense of play that had come so easily to Walker.

Oh, Charity, I wish you'd have told me more about the man you'd married. Did you know he came from a large, extended family? Did he really abandon you?

There was so much left unsaid.

Time had run out for her and her sister. She would do better with her nieces. If they wanted a dog, she would find a way to get them a dog. It would mean moving out of her apartment in the city sooner than she'd planned. Finding a larger space near the university wouldn't be easy, as her initial inquiries had proved. Now she would have to broaden her search to include a pet. This was assuming she was able to keep guardianship.

Brent Evans was the unknown factor in the equation. *Solve for X*, she told herself, but she still came up empty.

Hope fired up her laptop and typed *Doctors Without Borders* into the search program. After a quick click through the various pages on their website, she found a personal diary penned by a doctor who'd caught Ebola on one of his tours. It was a pretty harrowing account.

Her heart filled with fear, for Brent, for the possibility that the twins could lose their father before they ever met him.

Her phone vibrated on the desk beside her. Hand shaking, she picked up the device and took a look at the caller ID. The name on the screen did nothing to erase her unease. Stepping out into the hallway, she pressed on the flashing green icon. "Dr. Evans?"

"Walker."

"Walker," she corrected. "Is everything all right? Have you heard from your brother?"

"Not yet."

Hope thought about the account of the Ebola outbreak she'd just read. "Is his silence something we should be worried about?"

"Not necessarily. It's only been a few hours, and the workday isn't over yet."

"That makes sense." Her research had barely skimmed the surface. The Doctors Without Borders website showed pictures from rural locales where regular medical equipment and modern sanitation were limited. But there were also photographs of doctors working with advanced technology. "What kind of physician did you say your brother was?"

"I didn't. He's an anesthesiologist."

That meant he worked in operating rooms with modern equipment. A portion of her concern evaporated. "I assume there's a reason for your call?"

"There is. What kind of pizza do the twins like?"

"You want to know their pizza preferences?" She couldn't explain why this surprised her, but it did. It seemed everyday and normal.

"Quinn put me in charge of providing dinner for tonight's gathering. I don't know how much your background check revealed, but if it came back saying I am a culinary genius, it was dead wrong."

His reference to her preparation for their first meeting—she refused to call it a background check—brought a flush to her cheeks. "They like cheese pizza."

"Seriously? Not pepperoni? Every kid I know likes pepperoni."

"Not Harper and Kennedy." Finally, there was something she knew about the twins no one else did. It was petty of her but, in that moment, she needed the feeling of control.

"What about you? What kind of pizza do you like?"

She sighed. There had been enough evasion and avoidance of direct answers for one day. "Pepperoni."

His soft chuckle did strange, warm things to her insides. She did not like the sensation, not one, tiny, little bit.

"Now that we've settled that," he said, clearly amused. "Let's discuss the rest of the evening."

"Good idea."

They agreed to let Hope do most of the talking. Walker suggested she keep the mistaken identity piece of her story to herself. "I'm not comfortable with that," she said. "Besides, won't your siblings notice the discrepancy on the marriage certificate and put two and two together?"

"Maybe, maybe not. Look, Hope, I'm not asking you to lie. I'm merely suggesting you gloss over the more unpleasant portion of the story. Your mistake is not important."

She disagreed. Brent had forged his brother's signature. It stood to reason Hope would have come after the wrong man. Clearly, Walker was trying to prevent her from any further embarrassment. Which was really sweet, but totally unnecessary. Hope took a different approach. "Weren't you the one who said a half-truth is a whole lie?"

"Look at you, using my own words against me. I bet you're a tough one in the classroom."

"You…" She wobbled unsteadily and had to brace a hand on the wall to regain her balance. "You know I'm a professor?"

"I did a Google search, *Dr.* Jeffries. You have a PhD in Economics and another in Mathematics, with an emphasis in Statistics. You share your considerable knowledge with both undergraduate and graduate students at Columbia University in New York City. I'm impressed."

There went her insides, turning all soft and warm again. "Don't be. I just like school."

"Apparently." His voice held admiration.

"Was there anything else?"

"Nope. We're done." He disconnected the call before she could respond.

Staring at the blank screen, Hope stepped back into her hotel room and moved closer to the edge of the bed where the twins slept. They looked so peaceful. They'd suffered so much upheaval in their short lives. She wanted to provide them with stability.

She'd dropped them in the middle of more chaos, instead.

Filled with regret, Hope moved to the window and glanced out over Main Street. Christmas had exploded on the streets of Thunder Ridge. What child wouldn't love living here?

Deep-rooted longing filled her. Out of necessity, Hope had learned to rely solely on herself. As a kid, she'd become an island in a sea of rotating homes and faces, good people helping out their beloved, grieving pastor. They'd opened their homes to Hope and Charity, but only temporarily and never for longer than a year, maybe two. Always a new beginning that never lasted.

The twins would not experience that level of uncertainty. They would always have Hope. She would not be pushed out of their lives.

Time to put Plan B in place.

She went back to her computer and composed an email to her department chair. Then she began another Google search, this one to secure her future with the twins.

From his vantage point on the porch, Walker watched Hope's rental car turn into the drive. He waited until she pulled to a stop behind McCoy's Jeep before leaving his perch. He crossed the distance at a deliberately casual pace. He hated the idea of Hope and the twins staying in a sterile hotel room. That was a conversation for another time.

The twins spotted him from the back seat. They waved frantically. He returned the gesture, his heart kicking against his ribs as they scrambled out of the car. Hope had dressed them in their red coats and jaunty caps again. She herself had donned fancier outerwear than what she'd worn this afternoon. This one was made from green wool that matched the color of her eyes.

She'd left her hair free so that it hung in long, unruly waves past her shoulders. As was her habit, she absently hooked a few curling strands behind her ear. The gesture sent his gut rolling into a tight knot.

The masculine interest felt foreign. It made him itchy, like his skin didn't fit quite right. Walker shouldn't be this intrigued by a woman, by any woman, but especially not one he could be facing in a courtroom in the near future.

Harper and Kennedy called out to him, their grins wide and full of joy. Standing next to their aunt, the trio looked like they were ready for a holiday photo shoot and, despite knowing the danger of opening his mind to the possibility, Walker envisioned a different future for himself. Something more than returning to an empty house after a long shift in the ER.

He pushed the image aside. "Here you are, the three prettiest ladies in town."

The girls giggled.

Hope remained silent.

"I like it here," Kennedy said, gaping at the house behind Walker. "It's so pretty."

Walker glanced briefly over his shoulder, considering the house from an outsider's perspective. "My sister dresses up her home for all the holidays, but Christmas is her very special favorite."

"What other holidays?" Hope asked, her eyes nearly as wide as the twins as she gazed at the house.

"All the big ones. Valentine's Day, St. Patrick's Day, Easter, Fourth of July, Founder's Day, Oktoberfest, Thanksgiving and…" He took a breath. "I think I missed a few."

"So many?" Hope's eyes were slightly misty

as she spoke. Her emotional reaction seemed to hold a kind of longing that didn't fit with her polished facade.

Walker wished he knew more about her. His internet search had been short due to time constraints. He'd found her curriculum vitae from two years ago, but she wasn't on any social media. He'd located a few images of her at various black-tie events related to the university where she worked, but not much else.

"This house is the bestest of all the others we passed," Harper said, her voice filled with little-girl awe.

Walker attempted to take in the house with fresh eyes. Sitting on five acres of prime Colorado real estate, the rambling two-story house was nestled on the banks of Thunder Ridge Lake and had the quintessential wraparound porch. Quinn had decorated the exterior tastefully, but with what Walker considered a heavy hand.

Thousands of white twinkling lights—*not* an exaggeration—hung from every roofline and easement. Illuminated wire reindeer fed on a blanket of snow. And that was only the beginning. "The inside is just as amazing as the outside."

"I can't imagine." Walker heard the faint wonder in Hope's voice as she pulled out her cell phone and took a photo, then several more. "You're fortunate to be a part of all this."

She swept her hand in the general vicinity of the house. Once again, he regretted not digging deeper into Hope's past. His need for information hadn't been strong enough for him to invade her privacy any further. Walker hoped he hadn't made a mistake. Two little girls' futures depended on him knowing everything he could about their aunt.

Had she been given the love and security that came from strong family ties? Hope could prove herself a woman who didn't value family. He dismissed the thought. Her devotion to the twins was too strong, too genuine.

The front door swung open and the entirety of his family spilled out onto the porch, including dogs and a cat Walker had never seen before tonight. "Looks like the gang's all here."

"I…oh, my." Hope fell back a step. "I knew there were a lot of you. I just didn't realize there were *so many* of you."

Walker smiled to himself. Rachel had been equally blown away by the sheer number of Walker's family members. She'd eventually gotten used to it, but it had been touch and go for a while. They'd even discussed moving away, which had been a source of contention between them.

The thought felt like a betrayal to his wife's memory.

He eyed the Evans clan, which included two of

his three brothers, Quinn's husband, Grant, both sisters and a collection of mangy dogs running around his twin nieces, Bertha leading the pack. The only animal missing was Quinn's dog, Daisy, a pug-beagle mix that had recently given birth to a litter of puppies. "We're pretty overwhelming at first. But we don't bite."

"If you say so."

He gave Hope's hand a reassuring squeeze, then turned to the twins. They were clutching onto Hope with wide, uncertain eyes. Their inherent shyness had kicked in. Walker decided to ease the next few moments for them, and their aunt. "Wait here."

Leaving the twins with Hope, he hustled toward the porch.

Quinn met him at the bottom of the steps. "What's up?"

"The welcome committee is a bit too much for the twins."

Quinn glanced over her shoulder. "I didn't think. I was just so excited to see them again."

"I understand." Walker had felt the same way. "How about we hold off on the introductions until after the four of us enter the house?"

"Good idea." Quinn started ushering everyone inside. Skylar and Sinclair weren't as agreeable to the change of plans as the rest of the family. "But we want to meet Walker's friends now."

He breathed a sigh of relief, silently thanking Quinn for holding off telling the family too much about the twins.

"You'll get to meet the girls soon," their father said, glancing at Walker, who gave him a short nod.

Quinn picked up the conversation from there. "Let's think of a way to entertain the twins while we wait for the pizza to arrive?"

Two little faces scrunched in concentration.

"We could show them the puppies," Skylar suggested.

"And maybe we can put pretty ribbons on them," Sinclair added. "You know, dress them up a little."

"I have just the thing in my bag." His sister Remy, the family's resident veterinarian, said. "Come on, I'll show you."

Remy and Quinn led the twins inside the house. Grant followed a step behind the women, Casey one step behind him, his matching pair of English bulldogs hard on his heels. When McCoy attempted to bring up the rear, his hand on Bertha's harness, Walker stopped him. "Hold up. Can I borrow your dog?"

McCoy's brows went up.

"The twins like her."

"Yeah, sure." He patted the animal on her head. "Be a good girl."

Bertha gave him an insulted doggie glare, as if saying she was always a good girl.

To his relief, the dog proved the perfect transition from car to porch. The twins were still petting Bertha when Quinn popped out of the house with her mom-smile in place. "Hello, girls. I see you like dogs."

They nodded.

"Do I have a treat for you." She reached out to them. They took her hands without hesitation.

Quinn paused at the front door and captured Hope's attention. Walker glanced at her, as well. Everything in her seemed a little deflated. As if reading her trepidation, Quinn smiled softly. "Our dog just had puppies."

The girls' squeals of delight drowned out Hope's response. Walker didn't need to hear her words to interpret the signs of defeat in her downcast eyes and slumped shoulders.

Clearly, he and his siblings had won this round. They were one step closer to bringing Harper and Kennedy into the family fold.

This was what Walker wanted.

They why did he feel like a world-class heel?

Because the twins were also a part of Hope's family. Impulsively, he reached for her hand then thought better of it. "Ready to head inside?"

She heaved a sigh. "Ready as I'll ever be."

Chapter Seven

Hope followed Walker inside the most perfect home she'd ever seen. Not magazine cover–worthy, but in a welcoming, come-inside-and-relax sort of way. She wanted to drink it all in at once. Her arms suddenly felt limp and her feet turned into heavy, clumsy blocks. She tried to focus on her surroundings, but she didn't know where to look first.

The house was at least a century old, probably built by some mining baron during the gold rush. The original woodwork gleamed, proving it had been given great care through the years. The scent of lemon wax and freshly baked cookies reminded Hope of her favorite temporary home. Mrs. McClain had been older, sweet and patient, and had taught Hope how to cook.

Quinn had decorated the interior of her home with as much abandon as she'd applied to the exterior. Crimson and gold dominated. Poinsettias lined the entryway and the sweeping stairwell that led to the top floor. Bowls filled with ornaments sat on end tables, garland hung on the doorways. And was that…mistletoe? She would make sure to steer clear of that.

"The others will already be in the kitchen," Walker told her, his voice distant, as if he was speaking at her through a wall of water. "This way."

He led the way down a hallway lined with an assortment of family pictures. Hope counted three Christmas trees along the way. Two of them carried the red-and-gold theme. But the tree standing in the corner of what looked like a children's playroom was decorated with less attention to order. A kids' tree. Hope nearly stumbled, wishing for something she'd never had.

Walker seemed to notice her mood change. He took her hand, his hold firm and supportive and somehow exactly right. "It's going to be okay."

The soothing words filled her in a rush and what had been a terrible moment was shoved into the past, already forgotten. "You better be right."

"I am." The words were spoken with such confidence, and without an ounce of arrogance, that Hope found herself smiling.

In the next instant, they were entering the kitchen. It was another large, homey space with granite counters, shaker cupboards and a backsplash of white subway tiles. The scent of baking cookies hung in the air.

Hope barely had a chance to take it all in before Walker began the introductions. "You've already met Quinn. And my brother McCoy. This is Casey."

The man nodded. He had the Evans eyes, but his hair was two shades lighter than Walker's.

Walker introduced Quinn's husband next. Grant Holloway looked every bit the high school principal he was, from the tortoiseshell glasses, khaki pants and polished brown shoes to the blue shirt under a dark brown argyle sweater vest.

The final person in the room introduced herself. "I'm Remy, the youngest in this massive brood. And before you say anything, I know what you're thinking."

Hope doubted that very much.

"You're thinking, isn't Remy usually a boy's name? Well, not necessarily. In my case, Remy is short for Reims, aka my mother's favorite city in France. And..." She shook her head, laughing softly. "That was probably way more information than you wanted to know about me."

Hope attempted a smile at the self-deprecating remark but came up short.

It's over, she thought with bitter grief.

By sheer numbers, the odds were in the Evans

family's favor. If they chose to form a united front, Hope was doomed. She'd known coming to Colorado had been a risk, but now that she was confronted with the reality of this big, large, tight-knit family, she felt like a David up against a formidable Goliath.

"Hey now, there's no need to look so deflated." As if to prove they were allies rather than enemies, Quinn slid her arm through Hope's and said, "We're all on the same side here."

Bold words, but Hope could feel the twins slipping away. "And what side is that?"

"Your nieces. Or rather—" she pitched her voice for Hope's ears only "—*our* nieces. We're in this together."

Walker had uttered similar words.

"Anyone gonna tell us why we're here?" McCoy glanced from Hope to Walker to Quinn, then back to Walker. "And why those little girls look so much like you?"

"I'll let Hope explain."

Extricating herself from Quinn's hold, Hope began at what she considered the beginning. "I met Harper and Kennedy ten months ago when my sister, Charity, their mother, showed up on my doorstep out of the blue. I had no idea of their existence before that day."

"Wait." Remy pushed away from the counter

she'd been leaning against. "You didn't know your own sister had given birth?"

"I'm sorry to say, no." Hope sighed. "We were estranged."

"That's rough." Remy looked around the room, held a few gazes, before zeroing in on Walker. "Siblings should be able to work through their differences, wouldn't you agree?"

"Let her finish the story. Go on, Hope. Continue," Walker said.

Not quite understanding the undercurrents between brother and sister, she kept to the basics. She glossed over the details of Charity's decline in favor of focusing on what she knew about the Las Vegas wedding and the twins' birth a little over nine months later.

"I found these two items in my sister's belongings just before her death." Hope passed around the marriage certificate and wedding photo. "When I confronted Charity, she admitted that the man in the photograph was the twins' father."

Silence fell over the room as one by one the Evanses took turns studying the marriage certificate then the picture. McCoy was the first to notice the discrepancy. "Hold up. The name on the marriage certificate says Walker Bartholomew Evans, but—" McCoy snatched the photograph out of Casey's hand "—that's Brent in the photo."

Casey snatched the picture back, studied it

a moment and then shook his head. "Oh, man. That's definitely Brent. And the woman looks like—" he zeroed on Hope "—you?"

"My identical twin."

Remy took the picture next. She already had hold of the marriage certificate. "What was he thinking signing Walker's name instead of his own?"

"I have a good idea," Walker said with a wry twist of his lips. "As I'm sure the rest of you do, too."

Six heads bobbed up and down.

Hope had no time to wonder what that meant. Walker was speaking again. "Only Brent can explain what was truly going on in his head at the time."

"So, question." Leaning back against the counter, Remy captured Hope's gaze. "If Brent led your sister to believe he was Walker, whose name is on the twins' birth certificates?"

Heat spread through Hope. There it was. The question she'd been dreading. She was about to lose the bargaining chip she had if this went to court. Hope had managed to convince herself she could keep the information to herself.

But now, with six pairs of eyes on her, she knew she couldn't withhold the truth any longer. "Charity didn't provide the father's name on the birth certificate."

"She left it blank?" Remy asked.

Hope nodded, feeling the same draining away of energy she did every time she looked at the documents. She expected an interrogation from Walker, but he only looked at her with a curious sort of silence, as if he was trying to figure out her angle.

"Is there any doubt Brent is the father?" This, from McCoy.

How she wished she could say yes. She rattled off the twins' birthdays, then after they did the math added, "You've seen them. What do you think?"

"I think I have a pair of adorable nieces," Remy said. The others agreed with equal wonder and, to Hope's sorrow, enthusiasm. This was not the reaction of a family that would just hand them over to a woman from New York.

"Has anyone attempted to contact Brent?"

"I've reached out several times," Walker said. "So has Quinn. He's not responding."

McCoy shook his head. "Let's see if he'll answer me."

"Or me," Remy said.

Cell phones appeared in rapid succession. Texts were sent. Calls were made, all of which went straight to voice mail.

While the siblings concentrated on their individual devices, Quinn pulled Hope away from the others. "Something's been bothering me all afternoon."

Hope flinched. "Go on."

"There's no way you could have known that was Brent in the picture. That means you thought Walker was the twins' father."

Heat rushed through Hope. "I did, yes."

Quinn's expression softened. "Let me apologize on my brother's behalf."

"That's not necessary, really. Once we sorted out my mistake, he's actually been pretty great." Walker could have been difficult. He could have blocked her from getting in touch with Brent.

He still could.

But now that all the siblings were involved it would be harder.

Hope took that to heart as the flurry of cell phone activity came to an end.

"Well," Remy said, amusement in her voice. "We certainly gave Brent something to think about. Poor guy won't know what hit him."

Poor guy? The man had abandoned his pregnant wife. He'd chosen to serve in a country of strangers instead of taking responsibility for his family. Hope's father had done the same, leaving her and Charity in the care of others while he flew halfway around the world to minister to lost souls.

Walker brushed her arm with a whisper-light touch. "You okay?"

"Don't be nice to me."

"You'd rather I be cruel?"

"I'd rather... I need a moment."

She tried to turn and go. He caught her arm. "Wait. Let's see if Brent responds to any of us."

And when he did, it would be the beginning of the end. Why had she come here?

This tangle of feeling in the pit of her stomach was grief. "Please, Walker, let me go. I need to be alone right now."

"Go on, then." He lifted his hands in the universal show of surrender.

Free at last, she rushed out of the room.

Walker gave Hope ten minutes to pull herself together. He used the first five to formulate a plan for telling Brent about his daughters. The siblings agreed that, no matter which of them Brent contacted first, the news should come from Hope via Walker. They also agreed to hold off telling the twins about their father. That, too, should come from Hope. Or possibly Brent. How he responded to the news would determine which of them would do the talking.

Satisfied with the plan, Walker found the twins playing in the basement with Sinclair, Skylar and eight squirming puppies. They didn't notice his arrival, which gave him the opportunity to watch them without interruption.

What he saw sent a wash of relief through him.

No longer looking lost and overwhelmed, Harper and Kennedy were laughing and kissing puppies and generally behaving like normal five-year-old little girls. The similarities between the pair of twins were obvious, mostly in the eyes, all four had Evans eyes. But where Grant had passed on his brown hair, Harper and Kennedy had inherited Brent's blue-black hair.

Kennedy picked up one of the puppies and buried her face in the furry neck. The gesture was so similar to the way Brent had reacted to his first dog that Walker found himself blinking in surprise. The girls really were Brent's daughters.

Satisfied the twins were in good hands, Walker went in search of Hope. He found her standing beneath the vaulted ceiling staring into the flames snapping in the hearth. Her hair took on the fiery colors. Seemingly lost in thought, she looked up at the Christmas tree. Tears had collected in her eyes, but none had spilled over. Bertha sat beside her, gazing up at her with adoration as she accepted Hope's gentle strokes.

Walker felt his own eyes burn at Hope's raw, uncensored look of grief, as if she'd lost her way and didn't know what came next. He knew that feeling, had lived with it for too many years to count on one hand. He approached her slowly, drawing to a stop on the other side of the dog. She looked over at him and their eyes met. The impact nearly threw him back a step.

How he wanted to reach to her, to comfort and soothe. And there, in the wanting, was an utter sense of betrayal for everything he'd ever felt for Rachel. In all these years since her tragic passing, Walker had never wavered in his loyalty to the vows he'd spoken in front of God. Until now.

Until Hope.

A tear wiggled to the edges of her eyelashes. He automatically reached to wipe it away but dropped his hand just as quickly. "You okay?"

"No." She swiped at her eyes with a single, furious brush of her fingertips. "But I will be, eventually."

He wasn't sure he believed her.

They continued staring at one another. "I checked on the twins. They're neck-deep in puppies and about as happy as I've ever seen two little girls."

"I'm glad." She continued stroking Bertha's fur, as if the connection with the dog somehow grounded her.

Walker felt a crack slit through his heart. He suddenly wanted to know everything about this woman. Her past, her present, her plan for the future.

Why her, Lord? Why now?

He wasn't ready to let Rachel go. But in that moment, he needed to comfort Hope more than he needed to hang on to the past. "We aren't going to take the girls away from you."

"You can't make that promise."

Maybe not. If she took this battle to court, Hope had a claim. She'd been the twins' custodian for months.

Not if Brent steps up. Not if we form a united front against her.

The thought of becoming her adversary made him sick.

"You should know, Walker—" Hope pivoted to face him directly, her expression fierce "—if my sister was right about Brent, if your brother abandoned Charity and the twins, I will not hesitate—"

"You don't want to finish that statement."

She pressed her lips tightly shut. Mutiny burned in her eyes.

"We aren't at war, Hope. We both want what's best for *our* nieces." He emphasized the word to remind her they were on equal footing. "You can't know what Brent did or did not do until we speak with him."

"Are you that confident he's innocent? Can you honestly say my sister lied about him?"

"I know my brother. He wouldn't have abandoned his pregnant wife."

Her bottom lip began to tremble. "Are you certain?"

"Yeah, I am."

"It's been a long day," Hope said, her tone defiant. "The girls and I should go back to the hotel and—"

"You need to eat."

"Yes, we do." She conceded. "But once the twins eat, we're leaving."

She didn't trust him, he got that, and she definitely didn't trust Brent. Hope only knew what her sister told her. Perhaps Walker could provide some clarity. "Come, sit for a minute. I want to tell you a story." He sat in a wingback chair, indicated she take its match. "It's about Brent and what he was going through when he married your sister."

Hope sat in the chair, Bertha's chin resting on her lap. "I'm listening."

Walker took his time organizing his thoughts. Retelling Brent's story would mean revisiting his own loss. That both he and his brother had suffered losses so close to one another had been a cruel twist of fate that should have brought them closer. If not to each other, then to God. Instead, Brent and Walker had turned their backs on one another and the Lord. "It happened over six years ago."

"What happened?"

"The accident."

Hope's eyes widened, but she didn't interrupt. Walker appreciated that. It gave him time to push aside the images bombarding his mind. Rachel writhing in pain in the ER. Her insistence the doctors focus on the child in her belly, instead of her. If Walker had refused, if he'd focused on Rachel, then maybe—maybe—he could have saved both his wife and daughter.

He shut away the memories.

"Brent had just finished his residency in anesthesiology." Walker left out that he had been too caught up in his own grief to welcome his brother home. "He'd returned to Thunder Ridge to marry a woman he'd known since childhood. Brent and Nicole and their group of friends from high school were avid rock climbers. The weekend before the wedding, they went on a climbing trip."

A gasp slipped out of Hope.

"I won't get into the details, that's Brent's story to tell. His fiancée and another woman fell from a considerable height. Nicole died in the ambulance on the way to the hospital. The other woman recovered, but she was left with a permanent limp. Brent blamed himself."

Walker had understood his brother's need to take responsibility. He'd done the same after Rachel's death. The guilt still clung to him today, always there, at the edges of his consciousness.

"Was the accident his fault?"

"There was an investigation. Turned out the rope had been made of faulty material. Brent was exonerated of any blame. But Nicole was still gone."

"That's tragic."

"There was a lawsuit. But Brent wanted no part of that. He said it wouldn't bring back Nicole."

Walker stared into the fire, remembering his brother's pain and the helplessness he himself had felt when he couldn't seem to set aside his own grief to help Brent through his. Walker simply hadn't tried hard enough. He knew that now.

He had words of apology to say to his brother, if only Brent would call him back. "My brother went a little wild after the accident."

"Wild, like taking impromptu trips to Las Vegas?"

"Apparently. Brent would disappear for days at a time, then show up full of remorse and determined to get his life back on track. But then the cycle would begin again. This behavior went on for months."

"I think I understand."

Did she? Walker wasn't convinced. "You've

met my family so you can figure out how we reacted. We called in the pastor from our church and, with his help, attempted an intervention. Which only managed to push Brent further away. Then, suddenly, after an exceptionally long binge, he called a family meeting and told us he'd signed up to work for Doctors Without Borders. He left for Africa a week later."

As if trying to form a mental picture, Hope watched Walker closely. "How long ago was this so-called epiphany?"

Walker did a quick mental calculation. "A little over five and a half years ago."

Her hand stilled on Bertha's head. "No mention of a Las Vegas wedding before he left, an annulment, anything?"

"No. Nor was there any mention of your sister or the possibility of a pregnancy."

"He may not have known Charity was pregnant," Hope conceded in a small, strained voice. Her reluctance at the admission was evident in her tight shoulders and pinched expression.

"Look, Hope, we could spend the rest of the evening jumping to conclusions, but I'd rather we didn't."

She looked ready to argue the point.

Walker didn't give her the chance. "Brent will respond soon, and then we'll know more."

"You seem certain he'll call."

"The family blew up his phone. He'll know something's up."

Hope let out a breath, sucked it in again, then slowly nodded. "I hope you're right."

"I usually am."

She smiled.

He smiled back, deciding it was best not to dwell on his own doubts concerning his brother's behavior. Hard not to. Brent hadn't been in his right mind when he'd married Hope's sister. Walker prayed his brother hadn't done something unforgiveable, like knowingly abandon his pregnant wife.

But if he'd done just that? Then Brent would make restitution. Walker would insist.

Chapter Eight

Once again, Hope thought that Walker knew their nieces better than she did. She watched, eyes wide, mouth slightly open, as the girls each consumed a slice of pepperoni pizza, then devoured a second. When they reached for a third, Hope turned to Quinn. "Three slices? Is that normal?"

"They're five," Quinn said on a laugh, seemingly unconcerned the twins were gobbling down their food. Probably because her daughters were doing the same. "And…pizza."

Hope shook her head, opened her mouth, but Quinn was still talking. "Come. Sit with me on the porch swing a moment."

She hesitated.

"The twins will be fine."

"I know, it's just…" She was being overprotective. There were five other adults in the house. Including Walker, who currently sat between the two sets of twins, consuming a slice of pizza with as much gusto as the girls.

Grabbing her coat and gloves, Hope followed Quinn out onto the front porch. They sat together on the swing.

After a moment, Quinn broke the silence. "You're holding up well."

Amazing, how the other woman's understanding tone gave Hope the desire to let down her guard. "I never expected to become a mother, not so soon, anyway. Now? I can't imagine my life without the twins in it."

"What will you do when Brent comes home?"

"Are you sure he will come home?"

"Of course. That's why you brought the twins to Thunder Ridge, isn't it? To meet their father?"

Hope felt suddenly weak, and very aware of the cold moving through her. A cold that had nothing to do with the weather. "Honestly? I wouldn't have been able to live with myself if I hadn't looked for their father, knowing he was out there somewhere."

Quinn was nodding before Hope finished speaking. "That says a lot about your character."

They'd reached a tipping point. Hope sucked in a steadying breath and made her decision. No more evasions, no more half-truths or whole lies or pretense. "I haven't told you everything I know about my sister and your brother."

"I assumed as much."

Hope looked away, feeling a little sick to her stomach again. At some point in the evening, as she'd watched the family take in the news of Brent's marriage to Charity, as she'd seen the concern for their lost brother coupled with their obvious love and affection for him, Hope had begun to believe Brent was not the cad her sister had portrayed. At the very least, he was a man who deserved a chance to tell his side of the story.

"What aren't you telling me, Hope?"

She looked back at Quinn. "According to my sister, Brent knew about the pregnancy and that was the reason he insisted on ending the relationship."

"You're claiming my brother abandoned his pregnant wife?"

Hope gave a long sigh. "I'm not claiming anything. I'm telling you what my sister told me."

Another long sigh followed, this one from Quinn. "I pray your sister was wrong." She glanced off in the distance. "It seems we won't know until Brent makes contact."

Hope shifted on the swing and stared at the other woman's troubled profile. Had Quinn told her to jump off a cliff, Hope wouldn't have been more surprised. She did her best to park her shock. "You aren't immediately coming to your brother's defense?"

"I wish I could." She sighed again. "Brent wasn't in a great place before he left for Africa. He'd suffered a tragedy that changed him beyond all recognition of the brother I knew."

"You're referring to the accident that killed his fiancée."

"You know about that?"

Hope gave a slight shrug. "Walker—"

"—told you. Of course, he did."

"He thought it would help me understand Brent better."

"And did it?"

"Yes," she admitted. "I can't imagine the pain of watching—"

She was cut off by the sound of the front door swinging open.

Both sets of twins came rushing out of the house, all four speaking at once. Hope could barely keep up, but was pretty sure she heard the words puppies, ice castles and then…sleepover.

Clearly more competent at deciphering little girl chatter, Quinn held up her hand to stave off any further chatter. "Hope and I will discuss it."

"Oh, please, Aunt Hope," Kennedy begged, taking her hand and bouncing on her toes. "Please, please, can we sleep over?"

Hope thought her heart might explode with equal parts love and dread. *Look at them*, she thought. *So happy, so normal. And so totally en-amored with their cousins. Their family.*

Family. There was that word again, the one that threatened to rip the girls from her. "We'll see."

"That means no." The child's crestfallen expression made Hope feel even more like the enemy. She had a momentary falling sensation in the pit of her stomach.

"It means, I need to speak with your—" Aunt, she'd almost said aunt. "Miss Quinn and I will discuss it. Now go back in the house, please, so we can talk."

She waited for the girls to rush off, before addressing Quinn. "They don't have their pajamas or toothbrushes."

And Hope wasn't sure she should leave the girls overnight with strangers.

Not strangers. Family.

"We have extras of both."

Hope dragged her bottom lip between her teeth. "What if they get homesick?"

"Then I'll call you and you can come get them."

Dr. Stephens's words filled her thoughts. *If you want them to be normal children, then you have to let them experience normal activities.*

Hope closed her eyes, feeling completely out of her depth. The falling sensation in her stomach turned into a tidal wave of anxiety.

"We'll keep them safe," Quinn said, her tone

mother to mother, as if understanding the core of Hope's reluctance.

"I suppose it'll be okay, so long as you make sure they get to sleep at a decent hour and promise to call me if anything happens."

"Done and done."

"I'm staying at the Grand Palace Hotel, room 303. Walker also has my cell phone number."

"I'll get it from him before he leaves tonight."

And just like that, the sleepover was a done deal.

Quinn let Hope give the girls the good news. Their excited shouts brought, if she were being honest with herself, a moment of utter grief. Harper and Kennedy were already bonding with their cousins. And pulling away from Hope.

She felt a little lost as she watched the girls rush up the stairs.

Turning to speak with Quinn, she found Walker standing in his sister's place. "Oh." Her hand flew to her throat. "I didn't hear you come up beside me."

"I don't doubt it." He chuckled. "A bomb could have gone off and you wouldn't have heard the explosion over all that screaming. Those girls have a healthy set of lungs. I know these things, I'm a doctor."

She laughed in spite of the sorrow moving through her. "I should get back to the hotel."

"I'll walk you out."

Hope said her goodbyes after she and Quinn made plans to meet for lunch and the kid exchange at Latte Da, a local diner known for its gourmet burgers and fancy fries.

Was this to be her life, then, she wondered as she joined Walker in the foyer. Kid exchanges at restaurants or airports after small snatches of time with the twins?

She closed her eyes and tried to recall a Bible verse that would bring her a moment of peace. She recited one from Proverbs she had etched on a pillow back in her apartment.

Trust in the Lord with all thine heart; and lean not unto thine own understanding. In all thy ways acknowledge Him, and He shall direct thy paths.

Hope let the words sink in as Walker ushered her out of the house. She paused and stared up at him. Under the soft glow of the porch light, he looked like a man she could count on, steady and sure, and very masculine. Hope had been around good-looking men before, including less than an hour ago in Quinn's kitchen. But none of them had affected her breathing like Walker did.

Why did he have to mess with her breathing?

His gaze tracked over her face, sending heat through her limbs, making them heavy and full of tension.

Oh, no. No, no. No matter how good-looking

he was, or how he made her breath hitch in her throat or made her knees a bit wobbly, he was not the man for her. Too much stood between them. Or rather, two little girls stood between them, figuratively speaking. On the other hand, what if she allowed herself to dream, only for an instant? If things were different, could she see her and Walker becoming something more than adversaries? More than friends?

"Do you and the twins have plans for Saturday?"

For a moment she just stared at him, the what-ifs and possibilities vanishing in the cruel light of reality. She'd hoped to be back in New York by Saturday filing papers that would make her the twins' mother. Best-laid plans… "Not really."

"What do you say I take the three of you to the Ice Castles?"

She stared at a spot just over his left shoulder, trying not to notice how her pulse rushed in her ears. "When the girls mentioned Ice Castles, I thought they were talking about a movie."

"Not even close. It's a city made out of ice. McCoy and his team harvest tens of thousands of icicles daily. Then they hand place them to create sculptures, tunnels and, as the name implies, ice castles."

"Sounds like a complicated process."

"And completely worth a visit." He went on to explain in greater detail.

While he spoke, Hope pulled out her phone and began a quick search of the Ice Castles. The images were spectacular, especially the night views. "The girls will love this."

Walker leaned in to look at her phone. "I think McCoy took those pictures himself."

"He's very talented." Hope was losing her cool. With Walker's face inches from hers, his warm, woodsy scent was slowly reeling her closer.

Time seemed to stutter to a stop as she looked up at him. She yearned for something. She couldn't quite say what. To soothe, or maybe smooth away that hint of sadness that seemed a part of him. She nearly reached up to push a lock of hair off his forehead, then caught herself. Taking a not-so-subtle step back, she quickly put her phone away and continued down the steps toward her car.

"Hope, wait." Walker caught up with her, his long, ground-eating strides making quick work of the distance. "You never gave me an answer."

She paused. "To what?"

"The Ice Castles, you, me, the twins. Tomorrow night."

This caused her a moment of indecision. She should say no. She didn't want to say no. "Sure. Why not?"

A bark of laughter slipped out of him. "I'm overwhelmed by your enthusiasm."

"Sorry, I…" He moved a step closer and she temporarily forgot what she'd been about to say. "It sounds fun. No, really, don't raise your eyebrows at me. I'm actually looking forward to seeing McCoy's Ice Castles."

"Uh-huh."

Their eyes held one beat, two.

"I'm *super* excited." She gave him a big, toothy grin. "Convinced now?"

"Getting there." His gaze tracked across her face. There was a look in his eyes that made her breath hitch in her throat. A mix of masculine intent and secret sadness.

It was the sadness that called to her. She stepped closer and surprised them both by pressing her hand to his chest. Neither moved. They didn't speak. All that was left was the staring, and the sharp intake of a quick, unsteady breath.

Beneath her fingertips, Hope felt the rapid tripping of his heartbeat. Her own caught the erratic rhythm. She could close the distance between them without much effort. All it would take was a little stretch. A slight lift onto her toes.

"You won't regret it."

Hope blinked. It took her a moment to realize he was talking about the Ice Castles.

Her hand dropped away, but she couldn't seem to force her feet to move.

Eyes still locked with hers, Walker gave her a slow, careful grin. "I'm glad you brought the twins to Thunder Ridge, Hope."

"I'm not sure I am." She hadn't meant to stay that out loud.

"Don't go negative on me." He put a finger beneath her chin and applied light pressure until her head tipped back ever so slightly. "We're going to figure this out."

We. There he went again, acting as if they were a unit, a team. Feeling slightly off balance, she breathed in a slow, careful breath.

What was it with her and the chaotic breathing all of a sudden? She'd never had respiratory issues. It must be the Colorado air. Too thin for her New York lungs.

Fat, languid snowflakes floated around them, lazy, unhurried, creating a surreal, almost wistful feel to the moment. "Is it wrong of me to want the girls to miss me tonight, just a little?"

"I think there's something very right about wanting them to miss you."

Why did he have to be so understanding?

Her life was about to change dramatically, once again, as it had eight months ago. She wasn't any more ready now than she'd been back then.

Sighing, she glanced at the perfect house behind Walker, and thought of the close-knit family, the loving siblings. But what of the parents? Where were they? Did Harper and Kennedy have grandparents? "What about your mother and father? Are they no longer living?"

"They are very much alive and kicking. Happy and healthy, and enjoying an active retirement in Arizona as we speak."

Of course, she thought a bit bitterly. *Perfect grandparents to go with the perfect family.* She hadn't realized she'd said that out loud, until Walker corrected her. "Not perfect, none of us are."

It was her turn to raise her eyebrows.

He stood there a moment, steady under her gaze, then shook his head. "We've had our share of tragedy and loss."

Brent had. What about Walker? "Even you?"

He hesitated. His expression could only be described as devastated. "Especially me."

The two words came out raw and full of pain. His gaze turned troubled, matching the sound, and Hope had done that to him. She'd been quick to judge this family, this man, and she regretted her behavior. It was clear Walker had suffered a tragic loss. Her private detective had either failed to uncover this bit of information or had chosen not to tell her.

What did it matter now?

"Too much death," he muttered.

In that, they agreed. Hope had lost her sister. Brent had lost his fiancée. Walker had lost someone he'd loved. She wanted to ask who she was, and what she'd been to him, but Hope didn't have the right to dig into this man's private pain.

She was still trying to sort through her confusion when his hand touched the back of her neck.

Her breath stalled in her throat.

Was he going to kiss her?

She had her answer when he guided her head to his shoulder, then wrapped his arms around her. He said nothing, simply held her against him. A moment of solidarity passed between them.

Only a moment before, Hope had been trying to figure out a way to offer comfort to Walker. Instead, he was consoling her. She wanted to weep, and to let his strength wash through her.

What must it be like to rely on someone like this good, decent man, to know she wasn't alone? But Hope was alone, and this was only a moment.

Too soon, Walker set her away from him. But then he pressed his lips to hers in a quick, matter-of-fact kiss.

He stepped back, stuffed his hands in his pockets. "I'll pick you up sometime after three."

"I thought you said the best views were at dusk."

"I'm guessing you and the girls didn't bring your snow pants."

"We don't own snow pants."

"You'll want them for the Ice Castles."

Feeling a stab of uncertainty, Hope looked out into the darkened distance. She didn't like the idea of shopping with Walker and the twins. It made them seem too much like a family. "I can take the girls shopping after I pick them up at the diner. We'll have time."

"I'm sure you will. But I'm friends with the owner of The Slippery Slope. He'll give you a better deal if I'm with you."

Arguing any further would only make her appear petty, or afraid. She was neither. Okay, she was both, but Walker didn't need to know that.

"See you tomorrow, Hope."

She nodded, then climbed into her car and drove away. Two blocks later, she braked at a stop sign and pressed her fingertips to the spot where Walker's mouth had touched hers. It had hardly been a kiss, nothing more than a brief meeting of lips.

Then why couldn't she stop smiling?

Her hand went back to the steering wheel and she continued through the intersection.

Walker wasn't the first man Hope had kissed. She'd had romantic relationships, several of them. Only one had left a few scars in his wake, a fellow professor with a fondness for dating several women at a time. When Hope had discovered his unfaithful ways, she'd cut him loose.

She'd been angry for weeks, but then something odd had happened. She'd listened to a sermon online about forgiveness. The preacher's words had resonated and she'd realized Jeff wasn't worth the anguish. Bitterness would not live in her heart because of him.

If Walker turned out to be the same as Jeff, Hope wasn't sure she'd get over him that easily.

Chapter Nine

Feeling more alone than he had in years, Walker suffered a fitful night, alternating between wakefulness and sleep. It wasn't that his body was out of sync with the change in his work schedule, although that probably played a role. He'd spent too long reviewing that moment when he'd forgotten himself, his past, *everything*—except the feel of Hope in his arms. The kiss had been as natural as breathing, and more of a betrayal because of it.

At one confused point in the night, he dreamed he was back in the ER. Rachel was there, too, her belly swollen with his child, the stomach pains bending her over at the waist. Walker kept reaching for her, always coming up short and gasping awake. At which point he would try to recall her features. Again, he came up short.

He abandoned sleep hours before dawn. As he showered and dressed for the day, he rehearsed the upcoming conversation with Brent, over and over. Time passed by until his phone buzzed, startling him out of his thoughts.

Walker checked the screen, blew out a relieved puff of air. "Finally."

His relief was cut short as he studied the text. His brother had only responded to him, not the rest of their siblings. The message was short and pure Brent. How "important" are we talking here? 1—10.

Walker frowned, recognizing his mistake. In his desire to keep from spooking his brother, he'd failed to instill the proper amount of urgency. Time to rectify that.

Walker typed, Not life or death, but a solid 8.5. Call me. Now.

A series of dancing bubbles showed, proving that Brent was in the process of responding. Then…nothing. He'd stopped typing. Walker drummed his fingertips on his thigh. A second later, Brent's reply came through. Heading into surgery, which IS life or death. Will call when the patient is awake.

Which could be an hour or longer, hard to know with the little information Brent had provided. Same old evasive Brent.

Blowing out a hiss, Walker checked the time. Early, but not too early to text Hope.

She responded immediately. At least we know he's safe.

Walker blinked at the phone, surprised at her response and yet…not.

His mind traveled back to the moment he'd pulled her into his arms last night. There'd been nothing romantic in the move. She'd needed comforting and, truthfully, so had he. Walker hadn't thought past the need to connect with another human being. But as soon as he'd held Hope against him, his motives had turned foggy, his loyalties divided.

Restless, edgy, he prowled through the house, turning on lights, looking around with a critical eye. He'd bought the house a year ago but hadn't done much with the decor. This was supposed to have been his fresh start. But without Rachel, he simply hadn't had the desire to make the house a home.

He paused in the living room. The ceilings were high and vaulted, with thick wood beams and posts. At the center was a wood-burning, stone fireplace. The floor-to-ceiling windows facing the lake revealed an awe-inspiring view, but the room still lacked warmth.

What would Hope think of the place? Would she want to add frills, or large throw blankets and sturdy furniture? Maybe pictures on the wall and—

Walker stopped himself. How could he be thinking of one woman when he'd pledged his heart to another? *Rachel has been gone a long time.*

She died a lifetime ago, and yet it had only been a handful of years on the calendar.

It was long past time he let her go. Walker knew this. He understood how unhealthy it was to hold on to her this long. Rachel had been beautiful and kind, a pediatrician with a big, loving heart. She wouldn't want Walker living like this, half alive, moving through life on autopilot.

He didn't know how to let her go.

The process had already begun, he realized. He shut his eyes, desperate to call up Rachel's image. Again, nothing. Needing to see her, to remember, he went into his study and booted up his computer. He spent the next hour scrolling through pictures from their wedding, their honeymoon, the gender reveal party at Quinn's house.

The back of his eyes burned. He rubbed at them, clicked on the next image. His arm was slung over Rachel's shoulders. They looked so happy, blissfully unaware she would be dead three months later after a perfect storm of complications.

His phone buzzed.

Brent, it had to be. Happy for the distraction, he glanced at the screen. Not Brent, Hope. He couldn't talk to her right now.

Placing his thumbs on the screen, he started

to decline the call, then reconsidered. He didn't want to be alone with the past. He wanted to hear Hope's voice. Hand shaking, he moved his thumb and pressed on the screen. "Hey."

"So, I was wondering—"

"Brent hasn't called yet."

A pause. "Okay, good. That's actually why I called. I was wondering if you would consider having me there when you talk to him."

It was Walker's turn to pause.

"I can answer questions he may have about Charity and the girls."

Admittedly, it wasn't a bad idea. "What about the twins?"

"I don't pick them up until noon." She explained about the plans she and Quinn had made to meet at Latte Da, then added, "I can come to you."

Walker thought of Hope in his home and realized he didn't hate the idea. He actually liked it. But then his gaze landed on the computer screen, on Rachel smiling out at him. McCoy had taken the picture just as the wind had picked up, sending her long red curls in a flurry around her face.

As he stared at the photo, Walker felt distant from the man standing next to his wife.

That was another time, another life. He went hot, then cold, and the room started to spin. "No."

The word came out slightly tortured. "I'll come to you."

Twenty minutes later, he was standing in the empty hotel lobby, waiting for Hope to join him. She exited the elevator looking young, fresh and alive. So very alive. She smiled, and it was a really great smile. Something inside him came to life, something he thought dead. He forgot all about court battles and DNA tests.

His phone buzzed.

Hope caught up with him at the same moment he looked at the screen. "It's Brent."

Her eyes filled with nerves. "Aren't you going to answer the call?"

Answer the call. Right.

Walker directed Hope to a quiet alcove off the lobby. Satisfied they were alone, he pulled the phone up to his ear, then decided to put the call on speaker. "Brent," he said, his tone neutral.

"Walker."

Apparently, this was how brothers greeted one another after five years of limited communication. Accepting his share of the blame, Walker softened his tone and tried again. "How did the surgery go?"

"The patient lived. Look, Walker." Exasperation sounded in Brent's voice. "I have three more surgeries ahead of me. What's so urgent that you felt the need to involve the entire family?"

Brent sounded irritated. Yeah, well, so was he. Which explained why his words came out as clipped and angry as his brother's had. "How about we discard the chitchat and you tell me about your Vegas wedding to Charity Jeffries?"

A long, tense silence met the statement, then a slow hiss sounded through the speaker. "Ah, that."

Walker shared a look with Hope. "Yes, *that*."

"You're mad because I signed your name on the marriage certificate."

Not mad, confused.

But time was short and the whys behind Brent's behavior was for another conversation. "We'll talk about that later. For now, I need to know about the annulment. Whose idea was it, yours or your bride's?"

"We…hang on a minute." A series of mumbles followed the command, as if Brent had covered the speaker with his hand while he had a brief conversation. When he came back on the line, his voice was filled with impatience. "What did you want to know again?"

Walker forced down his own impatience. He chose his words carefully, ensuring he didn't lead Brent to respond in a way that could be held against either of them in the future. Or in a court of law. "Your marriage to Charity Jeffries," he said. "And the subsequent annulment. Walk me through it."

"Now?"

"It's important."

"You aren't going to let it go, are you?"

"Nope."

"Fine. We got married the same night we met. We pretty much realized our mistake a few days later, but we managed to hold it together for about a month, maybe a bit longer." Brent spoke as if he were under interrogation. "I was pretty shook up by the events of a night I could barely remember. I committed to cleaning up my act, for good this time. But Charity didn't much like the sober, responsible Brent. And, quite frankly, I didn't like how she was always looking for the next party. We agreed to end the marriage. The End."

Not the end, Walker thought. But he said, "So, it was a mutual decision to break up?"

"That's what I said, isn't it?"

Walker glanced at Hope, caught the momentary tightening of her mouth, as if she were deciding whether to challenge Brent's story or let him talk. Walker rushed to fill the silence before she could. "One more question."

"Fire away." Brent sounded resigned, and a little snarky. Walker figured he deserved the latter.

"Did you know your wife was pregnant when you ended your marriage?"

"I...wait, *what*? Did you just say Charity was pregnant?"

"As a matter of record, your wife gave birth to two healthy baby girls forty-one weeks and three days after the date of your wedding."

"Did you say *two* baby girls?"

"That's right," Walker confirmed, then pressed for answers. "You really didn't know about the pregnancy?"

"Of course I didn't know." The irritation was back in his voice.

The conversation went quickly from there, mostly with rapid-fire questions from Brent and equally fast answers from Walker. As would be expected from a man who was just finding out he was the father of five-year-old daughters, Brent wanted to know why he was only hearing about the twins now, were they healthy, happy, what were their names, where were they were now. And on and on.

The conversation turned somber when Walker told his brother about Hope, and her appearance in Thunder Ridge the day before—had it only been yesterday?—which led to the inevitable, "But what about Charity? Where is she?"

Walker saw Hope's mouth working and decided to let her take over the conversation. "My sister died three months ago. Cancer."

"I'm really sorry to hear that. She was a special

woman." Brent paused, then made a sound deep in his throat. "We weren't meant to be together, but I was lucky to know her."

There was no doubting Brent's sincerity.

"Hang tight, I'm about to send you a few pictures of your daughters."

They all fell silent as technology worked. A gasp sounded from the other end of the phone, and then Brent said the words that would change all of their lives. "I'm coming home."

Walker was glad, until he got a look at Hope. She'd turned a pale shade of green.

"I'll be back in touch once I confirm my travel plans," Brent said. "It may take a while."

"Understood." This was what Walker had wanted to hear. Then why wasn't he happy? Where was the relief? "I'll look forward to your call."

He was aware of his heartbeat as he disconnected the call, and the look of defeat on Hope's face. Eyes closed, she sagged against the wall behind her.

Walker reached to her.

As if sensing his attempt to touch her, she shook him off with a wave of her hand.

Silence fell over them, a silence neither tried to break. Her eyes opened at last and Walker could feel the metaphorical wall she'd erected. They were back to being strangers again. It made him feel as wretched as she looked.

He wanted to feel enthusiastic his brother hadn't known about Charity's pregnancy, but instead felt a weight of despair. Not for himself or for Brent, or even the twins, but for Hope. She'd been so certain Brent had abandoned her sister.

Looking at her now, seeing the defeat in her eyes, Walker knew—he *knew*—she'd come to Thunder Ridge with the idea of gaining custody.

Hope had lost. Brent was coming home. He hadn't mentioned anything about next steps once he arrived. He could turn out to be just like her own father. He could choose helping strangers living halfway across the world over raising his own daughters.

Hope allowed herself the luxury of wallowing in a moment of wishful thinking. She hadn't lost yet. But she wasn't any closer to winning, either.

"Hope." She couldn't look at Walker, not yet. "Stay through the holidays."

Surprised, she met his gaze and felt his struggle. He, too, wasn't sure what came next. She told herself not to care that they seemed to be on the same page, but she couldn't do that.

We're in this together. In that moment, she realized he cared about the twins as much as she did. And…

He'd been speaking. "I'm sorry, what did you say?"

"I'd like you to consider staying through the holidays. There's no telling how long it will take Brent to make arrangements to come home. It could take days, or possibly weeks."

"That long?"

"Depends on whether he's planning a temporary trip home, or something more permanent."

A lump lodged in her throat.

"We have a lot of great traditions here in Thunder Ridge. Aside from the Ice Castles, there's the Tree Lighting Festival, the live Nativity Play, the annual parade on Christmas morning. You get the idea."

Every one of the events he mentioned sounded amazing. "I can't think past your brother's return. If he refuses to step up and be a father to the twins, I will need to—"

"That's a conversation for later."

Was it? There were steps Hope needed to consider, decisions to make, whether she went with Plan A or Plan B or Plan C, D or E.

Walker appeared to be thinking through a few plans himself. His next words confirmed her suspicions. "From everything you've said, I get the impression Harper and Kennedy haven't experienced a Christmas like the one Thunder Ridge puts on."

The twins weren't the only ones.

Hope smiled politely, ignoring the way Walker was looking at her with that infuriating mix of surety and challenge. "If we stayed—"

"I knew you'd see things my way."

"*If* we stayed," she began again. "That would mean at least three weeks in a hotel. I'm not sure that's a good idea for the girls."

As soon as the words left her mouth, she regretted them. There were a lot of other places for the twins to stay besides a hotel. Quinn's house, for example. Hope should have come up with a better excuse. Now she would be alone for the holidays, or mostly alone, on the outside looking in. It was her childhood all over again.

"I have another idea."

She just bet he did. But would it include Hope?

"The three of you can move into my house. No, don't say anything. I'm not through. Let me finish. There's plenty of room. I live on the lake just two houses down from Quinn, close enough to walk, even in the worst of weather."

"No."

"Why not?"

There were so, so many reasons. "The twins and I couldn't possibly stay in your house with you living there as well."

"Not at all what I meant. I'll move in with McCoy. You and the girls can have my house to yourselves."

Hope ignored the little flutter in her stomach, the one that wanted to experience everything Thunder Ridge had to offer, not just for the holidays, but for a lifetime. "You would do that for us? You would move out of your own house?"

"Consider it already done. What do you say? Want to join forces and give the twins a family Christmas like they've never had before?"

It was a dangling carrot.

She looked into his eyes for any signs of ulterior motives. She found several. Of course Walker had ulterior motives. They both did. But he'd offered to join forces, which meant he didn't plan to cut Hope out of the Christmas festivities.

Oh, boy, this was bad. In a really good way, but also a very, very bad way. The twins deserved to experience a Christmas in this town. And Hope wanted to give it to them. But at what cost?

She should say no.

She prayed for guidance, instead, knowing it would be wrong of her to take the twins back to New York now. And so, she caved. "When can we move in?"

"Is now too soon?"

Despite her misgivings, she laughed. The man had a good sense of humor. She wished she didn't like that so much. "How about first thing tomorrow morning?"

His smile turned a little crafty. "You won't regret this."

She worried that she already did.

Chapter Ten

At half past three Saturday morning, Hope hustled the twins out of their hotel room. They'd been grumpy ever since she'd relayed the message that Walker was running late. Apparently, some important meeting had run longer than he'd expected. Now that he was waiting for them in the lobby, Harper and Kennedy had become darling little angels, talking nonstop about their new friends, Skylar and Sinclair.

Hope predicted they would be thrilled when they learned the Holloway twins were their cousins. And that more sleepovers were in their future. Tears blurred her eyes. She wanted to weep, possibly forever.

Still, this was not the future she'd envisioned for herself and the twins.

She ushered the girls into the elevator, while they continued to extol the virtues of the Holloway family. It took tremendous effort to focus on their words. Ever since making contact with Brent, Hope's mind had been running through next steps. At some point, Harper and Kennedy would have to be told he was their father. Hope was still undecided if that conversation should take place before he came home or after.

In the meantime, she'd taken action securing her own future, one that would keep her in the girls' lives a little longer, regardless of what Brent decided to do about his daughters.

The conversation turned to the newborn puppies. "They were so cute."

Hope wouldn't know. She'd been unable to drum up the courage to walk down the basement stairs. She'd been too afraid she'd leave the Holloway's home with a puppy in her possession. She'd always wanted a dog. But her apartment building back in New York didn't allow pets.

Of course, Plan B would solve that problem.

The elevator dinged their arrival to the bottom floor.

As expected, Walker was waiting for them in the lobby.

A small smile played across his handsome face. He appeared rested. His hair was in a bit of disarray, as if he'd run his fingers through the dark, thick mass more than once. Since when had Hope become a sucker for the disheveled look? Since meeting Walker Evans, apparently.

He wore dark-washed jeans that hugged his long legs and a light blue sweater that matched his eyes. The hiking boots on his feet were worn. Overall, there was a masculine, outdoorsy feel to him. Refined yet rugged.

And there went her heart, pinging again.

The girls rushed straight to him, no hesitation.

In a gesture that was becoming as familiar as the man himself, Walker crouched to their level and opened his arms wide. The twins flung themselves at him. Laughing, he pulled them close, kissed each of their heads, then set them back and rose.

He greeted Hope with a slight touch to her hand. That simple brush of fingertips was oddly intimate, and her mind sped back to their kiss the other night. She shoved the memory aside and followed Walker outside. Hope breathed in the fresh mountain air, then looked around for Walker's SUV. It was nowhere in sight.

As if understanding her confusion, he pointed down the street in a northerly direction. "I'm parked in front of The Slippery Slope."

Two blocks later, Hope paused on the threshold just inside the ski shop and glanced over the impressive collection of skis, snowboards, walking sticks, sleds, snowshoes and all the accompanying outerwear.

Apparently, the people of Thunder Ridge took their winter sports seriously.

She was still taking it all in when a man about Walker's age approached. He walked like an athlete. He had a tall, rangy build, spiky blond hair, and was really good-looking, in that skier sort of way. Hope was certain she'd seen him before. On a poster somewhere? A magazine cover?

Walker began the introductions. "Hope, this is Reno Miller. Reno, Hope Jeffries."

Hope recognized the name immediately. She tried not to gawk, but…wow. "You're Reno Miller!"

"One and the same." He punctuated his words with the lazy, flirtatious grin she had, indeed, seen on a poster. And the cover of every sports magazine known to man.

Reno had won five Olympic gold medals and two world championships. Some of the news outlets called him a national treasure. Others called him the bad boy of the slopes. "You're a professional downhill skier."

Reno's smile never wavered, but his eyes went blank, distant. "*Former* professional skier."

"Right. Sorry. I knew that." She only just remembered the news stories about the terrible crash that had ended his career. According to the reports, the man was lucky to be alive. "I didn't mean to—" she paused, worrying that anything she said would bring back bad memories "—gush."

He lifted a shoulder. "It happens."

"Probably more than you would like."

It was the right thing to say. His manner turned less distant and his eyes held that warm, friendly note again. "What brings you to The Slippery Slope?"

"Walker is taking the girls and me to the Ice Castles. Apparently, we are not appropriately dressed."

"Hmmm." Reno's gaze slid over her. His eyes held a teasing light. "I've got just what you need."

If Hope wasn't mistaken, Reno Miller—*the* Reno Miller—was flirting with her. And if Walker's scowl was anything to go by, he was not amused. Was he jealous?

She wasn't sure what to think of that.

Clearing his throat, Walker stepped between her and Reno, practically shoving his friend out of the way. "We're on a time crunch, man."

"Are you, now?" Reno's amused expression bounced between his friend and Hope. "Can't say I blame you." His gaze dropped to the twins. "And who might you be?"

"I'm Harper and this is my sister, Kennedy."

"Please to meet you, Harper and Harper's sister, Kennedy." Reno shook each of their hands, then, proving why he'd once been the darling of social media, spoke to the twins as if they were just as important as any adult. "You're going to want a pair of sleds to go along with your snow gear."

Two pairs of eyes lit with curiosity. "Really? Why?"

"For the tunnels. Way more fun on a sled. Come with me. I have the perfect ones in mind."

"Are they pink?" Harper asked him, taking the hand he offered.

"Please. What other color would they be?"

"Maybe purple?" Kennedy suggested, trotting over to his other side.

"My friends—" he divided a look between the twins "—I am about to hook you up with the best pink and purple sleds in town."

The next half hour was spent shopping for the proper gear to experience the Ice Castles. Much to Hope's amusement, Reno proved to be an outrageous flirt. Walker ran interference whenever the man got too cozy with her. It sent a little thrill through her every time he literally stepped between them.

Instead of being deterred by his friend's heavy-handed antics, Reno upped his game and told Hope embarrassing stories about Walker. It was apparently all in good fun, because the two finished by firming up plans for a day of snowboarding five days later.

By the time they left The Slippery Slope, Hope and the girls had changed into their new snow pants, ski jackets and sturdy boots. Walker carried the sleds to the car, one pink, one purple. After the four of them piled into the SUV, Walker kept up a running commentary about what they could expect at the top of the mountain. He interjected a few really corny jokes, which made the girls giggle and Hope roll her eyes.

They felt like a family, the four of them. An illusion Hope knew better than to let take hold of her heart. Brent would be home soon, and that would be the end of these types of outings.

Hope forced herself to make small talk. "How long have you known Reno?"

"Since before we could crawl. Our parents are best friends and have been for well over three decades. In fact, they retired near each other down in Phoenix."

Hope wondered what it must be like to have lifelong connections. Not to mention friendships that had started during your diaper days. "I liked Reno."

"I noticed."

Hope resisted the urge to laugh. "He's nice, but definitely not my type."

"No?" Walker gave her a sidelong glance. "What is your type?"

Men who are dedicated to helping others. Hope straightened in her seat. Where had that thought come from?

She glanced out the window, not really seeing the scenery as she answered his question. "I suppose I like them to be a tad more cerebral than the average bear."

"I've read *Moby Dick*, *Beowulf* and *A Tale of Two Cities*." He wiggled his eyebrows. "I also know all about Keynesian economic theory."

"Prove it."

He shot her a smug grin before returning his gaze to the road. "Keynes believed that consumer demand was the driving force in any economy. He supported increased government spending during recessionary times and government restraint during a rapidly growing economy."

"Well, okay then." Hope blinked. "That was pretty spot on. I'm impressed."

"Don't be." His lips twisted at a wry angle. "I looked it up on my phone while you were flirting with Reno."

"I was not flirting."

He lifted a brow.

"Okay, I was flirting, but only a little, and he started it. What can I say?" She tilted her head back to look into his eyes. "I'm a sucker for bad boys."

"I thought you liked them smart."

"A bad boy can be smart."

He considered this in silence as he turned onto another steep, winding mountain road that took them up, up, up. Distracted by the awe-inspiring view, Hope gave a short, happy gasp.

"Is that an eagle?" She pointed to a bird with a massive wingspan.

"A hawk. And that—" Walker nodded toward an animal grazing on a small ledge halfway up the rocky cliff "—is a mountain goat."

Hope eyed the creature with the massive twisting horns. "He's beautiful. It's all beautiful. Colorado is amazing."

"You are not wrong. Look, girls, the Ice Castles are just up ahead."

A chorus of delighted squeals rose from the back seat. Hope nearly joined in. Even from this distance, she could tell Walker had not been exaggerating when he'd claimed the sculptures were enormous. Some of the structures appeared to be several stories high.

"McCoy is a genius."

"He would tell you the same. Humble, he is not." Walker's tone was full of good humor as he steered the SUV through a wooden gate.

He'd barely parked before Hope was hopping out of the car.

As if they'd done this a million times, she and Walker helped the twins out of their car seats in the back. While she straightened their coats, he went around back and retrieved the sleds. Tucking them under his arm, he winked at the girls. "Ready to party?"

Hope directed the girls toward a ticket booth, but Walker stopped her. "Already taken care of. You forget, I have connections."

The man was nothing if not prepared. *A kindred spirit*, Hope thought, with a little twinge in her heart. She studied Walker out of the corner of her eye. A strange sensation washed through her, as if she was poised on the edge of something significant. Good or bad, she couldn't yet say.

With Walker guiding them through the entrance, she felt a part of something bigger than herself. Instead of overthinking it, a bad habit of hers, she resolved to enjoy this adventure with Walker and the girls.

If her brain wanted to do a little wishful arithmetic, making one plus one plus two equal a family of four, then she would go with it.

But only for today.

Once they passed through the entrance, Walker turned to Hope. "Prepare to be amazed."

"I already am."

"Do you have a dog?" Harper asked Walker.

He blinked at the random question, a distant look on his handsome face. "I used to. But not anymore." He seemed caught in a memory that brought more sadness than joy. "We're here."

The four of them stopped at the base of a working fountain made of ice. There was no more talk of dogs or puppies. The girls were too busy spinning in circles, looking everywhere at once.

Hope bounced her gaze past the fountain, to a group of animal sculptures, a miniature princess castle, a perfect replica of Santa riding his sleigh, then back to the fountain. "It's a whole world made from nothing but ice and water."

For the next hour they explored the frozen world. Walker encouraged the girls to touch one of the structures. They sat on kid-size thrones next. Then crawled through tiny ice tunnels, which earned them high praise from Walker.

At one point, he pretended to get stuck in a tight walkway. "We'll save you, Dr. Walker," the twins cried out. Taking their role as his rescuers very seriously, they tugged on his hand until he slid through the tight quarters.

Hope rode down a slide behind the twins, more than a little grateful Walker had insisted on the snow pants. She crawled through a tunnel lit by blue and pink LED lights. He caught her hand from the other side and pulled her through the final few feet. Her breath caught and a belly-clenching thrill rolled in her stomach.

"Look up."

Hope gasped. Thousands of icicles hung over her head.

They finished their journey where they'd begun. McCoy stood at the fountain illuminated with red and green LED lights, Bertha by his side. He was talking to a woman dressed in faded jeans, battered boots and a forest green puffy jacket. Her hair was a light, golden brown with plenty of blond streaks, shiny and thick, and just barely brushing her shoulders. She was also leaning heavily on a cane. "Who's that with McCoy?"

"That's Bertha."

"Not the dog, the woman."

"Emma Summerland."

"I didn't know McCoy had a girlfriend."

"She's not his girlfriend." Walker glanced at the twins, back to Hope, indecision in his eyes. Then he spoke. "Emma was on the rock-climbing trip with Brent."

Hope felt her heart sink. Emma Summerland was the other accident victim that had sustained a life-altering injury.

As they drew closer to the fountain, Hope studied the other woman. Emma was very pretty, gorgeous really, and appeared near her same age. Her manner was lighthearted despite the cane, as if she was happy with her life. Her sparkling eyes held no bitterness. They were a pretty shade of light green and, at the moment, full of curiosity.

Dividing her gaze between Hope, Walker and the twins, her eyebrows drew together. She appeared to be puzzling over the family resemblance.

Would everyone in town assume Walker was the twins' father, and that Hope was their mother? The thought brought a wistful tug somewhere in the vicinity of her heart. She liked the idea of her and Walker raising the twins together. Maybe a little too much.

Surely, she wasn't falling for a man she'd only just met.

"Bertha!" Kennedy's shriek rent the air.

Both twins ran to the dog without a second thought to their safety. Hope called after them to slow down, which was promptly ignored.

Walker chuckled beside her. "I think it's love."

"The twins or the big, furry dog?"

"All three."

Their eyes locked, held. A moment of silent understanding passed between them, something that was altogether theirs alone.

Hope looked away, and right into Emma's all-too-knowing smile. The other woman thought Hope and Walker were a couple. Hope should correct her assumption. Except...

How did she go about correcting a misconception that hadn't actually been voiced? She didn't.

As Walker made the introductions, Hope attempted a bland smile. A wasted effort. Emma's full attention was now on the twins. "Who's who?"

"I'm Harper." This was said absently. The child's focus was solely on the dog.

"That must make you Kennedy."

The little girl glanced up. "That's me."

Emma's delighted expression stayed hooked on the twins. "I really like your sleds."

Kennedy continued looking at her. "They're new."

"Even better." So began an extensive dissertation on their shopping expedition at The Slippery Slope. Kennedy did love her shopping trips.

Apparently, Emma did, as well.

Walker pulled Hope aside. "Emma is a kindergarten teacher at the Thunder Ridge elementary school."

Which explained her ease with the twins, and her ability to understand the storytelling of five-year-olds. As she watched the interaction, Hope stood rooted to the spot by a deep, undefined ache in her chest. If Brent won custody, the twins would attend school in Thunder Ridge. Emma would probably be their teacher.

Proving he just might have mind reading skills

after all, Walker took her hand. "It's going to be okay."

No, it wasn't. Hope's life was unraveling right before her eyes. She tried to pull her hand free, but she couldn't seem to do so. She didn't want Walker's comfort. And still, she held on to his hand, barely resisting the urge to cling.

She wanted to watch the twins grow into adults. She wanted to be a part of their lives every step of the way. She wanted to celebrate every triumph. Bandage every skinned knee, kiss away every hurt.

How, Lord? How do I let them go?

Chapter Eleven

Night had fallen by the time Walker drove down the mountain. The Ice Castles were nothing more than a collection of LED lights and sporadic shadows in the rearview mirror.

Walker could feel the turmoil rising in him. His connection to Hope was growing stronger, and more impossible to ignore. Even worse, he hadn't thought of Rachel at all throughout today's adventures. Guilt sent his heart thumping hard against his ribs and his palms sweating inside his gloves. *Set it aside*, he told himself.

Stay in the moment.

He glanced over his shoulder. The twins were talking to one another in low, excited tones. They were happy, exhausted and, according to Harper, really hungry. Walker made suggestions for dinner, mostly nicer restaurants.

The twins had their own idea. "We want to go to the Latte Da."

Walker turned to Hope. "Isn't that where you went for lunch today?"

Even in the dim light from the dashboard, he could see a dozen thoughts racing in her eyes, none of the happy variety. "It was a big hit with the girls."

"You don't mind going there twice in one day?"

"If the twins are happy, I'm happy." Her voice matched her somber mood.

Something was up with her, that much was clear. Walker wondered if she would confide in him, or if he would have to go on a fishing expedition. He would prefer she opened up on her own, so he waited for her to break the silence. And waited. And waited.

After a series of sideways glances in his direction, she turned her head to look out the passenger-side window. At last, she spoke. "I liked Emma."

An odd segue. Walker kept his answer neutral. "Most people do. Emma is a likable person."

"But—" Hope swallowed audibly "—is she a good kindergarten teacher?"

Yep, Hope had gone right where Walker guessed. Whether she admitted it out loud or not, she was already thinking about a future for the twins in Thunder Ridge.

Walker should be elated.

Hard to be when the sigh that leaked out of Hope carried an edge of defeat. He didn't want to win this way, not if it meant Hope had to lose. "I can't say what kind of teacher Emma is. Quinn would know. Her daughters were in Emma's class two years ago."

Nodding, Hope said in a slightly unsteady voice, "I'll definitely speak to your sister. It would help to know what she thought about…"

She turned to look out the window without finishing her thought. She didn't need to finish. Walker knew what she meant.

In that moment, he felt profoundly that he'd failed Hope. The sensation grew stronger when he considered the meeting with his attorney two days ago. Mitch had assured Walker that Brent had a strong case for custody. Especially if, as Brent claimed, Charity had kept her pregnancy a secret from him. And Walker believed his brother.

Hope seemed to be withholding final judgment until Brent came home. Once he did, would she dig in her heels on her sister's behalf, a woman who couldn't defend herself? Would it even matter?

This was a classic case of he said/she said, which gave Brent the advantage since he could make his case in front of a judge. Walker didn't want to be on the opposite side of Hope. He wanted to work with her, as he'd promised.

Set it aside.

He reached out in the darkened interior of the SUV and took her hand. He considered it a win that she didn't pull away for several life-affirming heartbeats.

Dinner was a combination of hot dogs, french fries and an enthusiastic revisiting of their recent adventure at the Ice Castles.

Heart full, Walker joined the conversation.

During a brief lull, he greeted the duo seated at the table next to theirs. "Wyatt." He nodded to the little boy with him, a child a few years older than the twins. "Samson. Wyatt is the newly elected sheriff in town," he added for Hope's benefit.

Hope seemed a little shocked.

"What?"

"Do you know everyone in Thunder Ridge?"

"Only the important people." He winked at Samson, who beamed back at him.

Walker was pleased to see the boy smile, a rarity since his mother, Wyatt's sister, had been found guilty of a felony drug charge. The whole ugly mess had been a big scandal in town, made worse because Wyatt was the arresting officer.

CiCi wasn't a bad person, just really lost after the death of her husband in the car accident she'd caused. A series of bad decisions had sent her down a path of self-destruction that had endangered her son. Samson was doing better now that he was living full-time with his uncle.

"We went to the Ice Castles," Harper told Samson with no small amount of pride.

"Did you crawl around in the tunnels?"

"Well, yeah." Kennedy rolled her eyes in a gesture filled with little girl impertinence. "Duh."

Hope gasped. "Kennedy, don't be rude."

The child looked completely unrepentant. "It was a dumb question, Aunt Hope."

Hope and Samson responded at the same moment. "No, it wasn't."

"Say you're sorry," Hope urged the little girl.

"I'm sorry," Kennedy spat out the words, while Hope, looking both distraught and embarrassed on her niece's behalf, gave an apologetic grimace to Wyatt.

Samson swung around, putting his back to their table, but not before saying in a voice loud enough to be heard three blocks over, "Stupid girl."

Now Wyatt looked distraught and embarrassed. "Samson! We don't use that word, ever. Apologize. Now."

Samson swung a scowl in Kennedy's general direction. "I'm sorry I called you a girl."

Wyatt sighed. "You know that's not what I meant. Try again."

"Fine. I'm sorry I called you stupid." The little boy growled out each word through clenched teeth.

Hope nudged Kennedy's shoulder. "Your turn. Say you're sorry, and mean it this time."

Arms crossed over her chest, the little girl gave her aunt the stink eye, then turned the same look onto Samson. "I'm. Sarr. I'm…sar." She huffed out a whooshing sigh. "I'm sorry."

The two children scowled at one another, accepting the other's apology with grudging nods. Hope and Wyatt apologized to each other on the children's behalf.

Walker did his best not to laugh, and managed to succeed, mostly. Except for a low snicker in the back of his throat, which earned him an adult version of the stink eye from Hope. He maintained his composure until the girls were secured in the back seat, with the SUV's doors closed behind them.

"What's so funny?"

"Kennedy and Samson." He gave his laugh free rein. "Priceless."

Looking ready to rumble, Hope's eyes narrowed. "I don't see the humor."

"Come on, Hope. Those apologies were funny, and you know it."

Her lips twitched. But she didn't give in to a laugh. "I don't know what got into Kennedy. She's never been rude like that."

"She was behaving like a normal kid." He moved in closer, feeling the tug of this woman as if they were tethered by an invisible cord. "Call your therapist and see what she has to say about it."

Hope's chin lifted at a haughty angle. "Maybe I will."

Walker was only half surprised she didn't pull out her cell phone and make the call right there on the street corner. Still smiling—he couldn't remember when he'd smiled this much—he dropped off the trio at their hotel. They made final plans for the big move the next day, agreeing mid-morning would work best.

That night, for the first time in months, maybe years, Walker entered his home with a woman other than Rachel on his mind.

The next morning, while the girls packed their suitcases, Hope stepped into the hallway and made a call to New York. She disconnected a few minutes later. Dr. Stephens had agreed with Walker's assessment about Kennedy's rudeness at the diner, calling it normal five-year-old behavior. Hope was relieved.

The twins had been entirely too timid and distant prior to coming to Thunder Ridge. The change to normal five-year-old behavior was a blessing she'd been praying for since they'd come into her life.

What worried Hope was that the girls' transformation could be directly attributed to their interactions with Walker and the rest of the Evans family. *Family.* There was that word again. She swallowed back a sob. And went back into the hotel room to finish her own packing.

"I can't wait to see Dr. Walker's house," Harper said.

Hope was equally curious.

"I wish he was going to live there, too."

Hope had already explained why that wasn't possible. Or rather, she'd given the girls an explanation that a kindergartener would understand. "We can't stay in the same house with a man we only met a few days ago. It wouldn't be appropriate."

"You could always marry Dr. Walker," Kennedy suggested. "And then he could be our daddy and you could be our mommy."

Hope's heart lodged in her throat. It was pointless to argue with five-year-old logic, especially when she didn't hate the idea as much as she should. She could picture the four of them as a family. She could picture being married to a man like Walker.

"Dr. Walker and I are not getting married." She said this as much for the twins' benefit as her own.

"Why not? You like him, don't you?"

"We haven't known each other long enough."

Harper and Kennedy shared a look full of silent twin messages. "Okay."

Okay? Hope blinked at the pair. When had either child ever given in that easily on, well, anything?

"If you won't get us a daddy," Harper said for the pair. "Can we have a puppy instead?"

More five-year-old logic that sent a ripple of frustration through Hope. "We'll see."

"Is that a yes," Kennedy asked. "Or a no?"

"It's a 'we'll see.' Now, if you're finished packing, it's time to go."

"We're finished." All conversation of fathers and puppies were dropped in favor of hurrying out of the room.

Twenty minutes later, Hope drew to a stop outside the address Walker had given her. She cut the engine and stared out at the massive two-story house overlooking Thunder Ridge Lake.

That is a lot of wood and glass, she decided, really enjoying the way the house seemed to merge with its rustic surroundings while still having a modern appeal. She could see herself coming home to a place like this after a long day of teaching.

As if she'd somehow called him with her thoughts, Walker exited the house and stood, hands stuffed in his back pockets, waiting for her and the twins. This is what he would look like if they were married and, and...

She stopped herself before she went any further

in her mind. Pocketing her car keys, she swiveled around to face the back seat. "We're here."

The twins fist-bumped, then waggled their fingers as they said in unison, "Firecracker!"

Hope's heart twisted. Walker had taught them the gesture last night. He'd become such a part of their lives. She tried not to resent that, and almost succeeded, but her mind kept circling around an irrefutable fact. Her life with the girls as she'd known it was coming to an end.

So little time left. Hope climbed out of the car, the twins right behind her. Walker went on the move, heading straight for her.

Her stomach performed a quick, hard roll at the sight of all that masculinity coming her way. He wore all black, save for the pristine white collar peeking out from beneath the neck of his sweater. His eyes were a pale blue under the bright sun. His smile a mere tilt of one corner of his mouth. Hope thought she detected a hint of humor in his expression, and something that looked like affection. For her, the girls, all three of them?

The responding tug at her heart felt too real. How was she supposed to remain immune to the man when he looked at her like…like…*that*?

"Good morning." His deep voice fell over her like a warm caress.

She had no time to respond before Harper was

tugging on his arm. "Aunt Hope says you can't be our daddy."

His gaze swung back to Hope. "Did she, now?"

"Yeah." Harper took a quick, audible breath. "But she said we can get a puppy, instead."

"I said we'll see."

"Okay, yeah," Harper admitted, engaging Hope in a stare-down that claimed she would not be denied this request. "But that's almost the same thing as yes."

Hope held the child's glare with an unflinching one of her own. "I made no promises, Harper."

Walker's chuckle interrupted the staring match. "Wise woman."

And now she was locked in a silent contest of wills with him. Their gazes held a long, silent beat. An unspoken message passed between them, but Hope couldn't quite decipher the meaning.

Walker broke eye contact first.

"Ready to move into your new home?" The words were directed at the twins, but Hope felt them all the way to the depths of her soul.

The words, spoken in that rich, masculine baritone, and the carefully constructed life she'd envisioned for herself with the twins morphed into something new. Something different.

And, for the first time in her life, unrealized dreams seemed possible.

Chapter Twelve

Walker tried not to look at Hope. He tried not to look at the twins, either. The moment he'd caught sight of all three exiting the rental car, his mind had focused on one word. *Mine.*

Except, they weren't his.

Harper and Kennedy belonged to his brother. And Hope, well, she had a life in New York. It would be unwise to think of her as anything beyond the twins' aunt. She'd agreed to stay through the holidays, nothing more, and only for the girls. Still, his mind wrapped around one, unrelenting truth.

It isn't long enough.

"Are we going inside now?"

Walker smiled down at Harper. "Let's go."

"What about our suitcases?"

"I'll get them later."

He led the way, first onto the front stoop and

then inside the house itself. Where was the trepidation of welcoming them into his home? Nowhere to be found, he realized with his second
jolt of the day. He'd bought the house barely a
year ago, with the idea of finally putting the past
behind him. He'd planned to start the next chapter in his life.

He'd clung to a series of blurred images and
hazy memories, instead.

His gaze hooked on Hope. Something inside
him shifted. Walker wanted this woman in his
home, in his life. The thought pulled him up
short. Ever since Hope had barged into his ER,
Walker had begun looking to the future instead
of dwelling on the past.

He glanced down at the twins. They'd played
a role, as well. "Let's get you out of your coats."

A lot of shuffling and giggling filled the next
few minutes as he and Hope removed the children's outerwear. The happy sound bounced off
the walls and landed straight inside Walker's battered heart. He heaved a weighty sigh and, determined to live in the moment, concentrated on
hanging the girls' coats on hooks near the front
door.

Hope rested a palm on the banister leading to
the upper level and looked around with an as-
sessing eye.

"Well?" he asked. "What do you think of my house?"

She checked herself slightly at the question, so slightly Walker almost missed it. "You really want to know?"

"I do." Her opinion mattered.

"It's nothing like my apartment. There's a lot of wood and glass, everywhere."

He glanced around, trying to take in the house from a woman's perspective. "Is that a problem?"

"Not even a little bit. My view in New York is of the building across the street. The girls and I have to walk five blocks to get to a park. But here? It's as if the architect managed to bring the outdoors right inside with us, while also maintaining a comfortable, welcoming feel."

Nice compliments, and yet he sensed she was holding something back. "But…?"

"The decor is a bit sparse. And I noticed yours is the only house on this side of the lake that isn't decorated for the season."

"I've been busy." It was a lame excuse even to his own ears, but she gave him a pass.

"No doubt. Anyway." She craned her neck to look past the foyer into the main portion of the house. From her vantage point, she could easily see into the living room, to the far wall made entirely of picture windows that looked out over the lake. "Whew. That's some view."

"One of the reasons I bought the house last year."

"You've lived here an entire year? Interesting."

He knew she had more to say, he could see it in her eyes. But she held silent for a moment. His impatience got the better of him. "Do you like the house, or not?"

"I think it's amazing. But, like I said, a bit sparse." She shot a significant look into the living room. "Christmas decorations would help."

He followed the direction of her gaze, pausing over a large empty space near the bay of windows. A Christmas tree would fit perfectly there. Some garland would be nice, too. Some of those twinkling little lights would add color.

"Do you have any available?" Hope wondered aloud.

"Sure, I do." He swung back around to face her. "They are currently sitting in one of those big-box stores waiting for me to purchase them."

As intended, she laughed. "Cutting it close, aren't you?"

"I have well over two weeks until the big day."

Hope tapped her wrist. "Ticktock, doctor."

He opened his mouth to defend himself, but the twins cut him off. "We'll help you decorate," Kennedy said, with Harper adding, "Yeah! It'll be fun."

"Consider yourselves drafted into service."

"Yippee!"

Walker smiled down at his two new recruits. Their joy was infectious. "Why don't you go explore your new home while your aunt and I retrieve your luggage from the car?"

"Can we, Aunt Hope?"

She gave her permission with a short nod.

The girls didn't need to be told twice. Off they sprinted, their shouts filling the empty house and, just like that, the crack in Walker's heart opened a little more.

"You just wait, Walker Evans. The girls and I are going to turn your house into a home this holiday season."

Home. The word rolled off Hope's tongue naturally, leaving Walker wanting something more, something he'd thought lost forever.

He wanted tomorrow.

He was actually reveling in the sensation, until Hope touched his arm and asked a question that killed his mood. "Any news from Brent concerning his travel plans?"

"Nothing yet."

Her eyebrows drew together. "I hate waiting."

Walker did, too, usually. Right now, he was a big fan of a nice long delay. Every hour Brent was held up in Africa was another hour Walker got to spend with Hope and the twins.

As if to mock him, the antique clock above the

fireplace chimed the hour. The sound reminded
him that time was running out. Or, as Hope so
eloquently said...

Tick, tock...

Due to a change in his work hours and other
scheduling difficulties, Walker didn't see the
Jeffrieses for the next several days. He'd texted
Hope, mostly to make plans to purchase a Christmas tree and other decorations for his house.
Hope had also agreed to meet him outside the
church building this morning, which happened
to be Sunday. He'd used the excuse that he'd
show her and the twins around, but he really just
wanted to make sure they sat with him during
service. He was starting to feel territorial.

That could be a problem.

And yet, here he stood, on the steps of Thunder Ridge Community Church, watching their
approach with his heart lodged in his throat. He
was reminded of the first time he'd seen the trio
moving toward him. He'd been struck speechless
by the sight they made, the very picture of the
kind of family he'd once craved.

The sensation was even stronger this morning,
because now Walker knew what he wanted. A
second chance at happiness. More than that, he
wanted the dream he'd nearly had once before.

A wife, a houseful of children, a few rambunctious dogs, all of it.

The twins caught sight of him first. They broke into a run and all but leaped into his outstretched arms. His greedy heart soaked in their joy. All too soon they wiggled out of his embrace.

"Will you sit with us?" Kennedy asked.

Walker smiled down at the little girl. "That's the plan."

He switched his attention to Hope. The harsh morning sun cast her in its stark glow, highlighting the purple shadows beneath her eyes. "Bad night?"

She looked ready to deny the gentle accusation. But then she shook her head and sighed heavily. "I tossed and turned," she admitted. "Any news from your brother?"

As if on cue, Walker's cell phone dinged. He thumbed open the message. "It's from Brent."

"What does it say?"

He allowed a brief silence to elapse, then looked up. He saw tiredness in Hope's eyes, and a shred of fear. "Read it yourself." Boarding a flight to Germany. Will contact you again when I land.

"So, he's officially on his way home," Hope said.

"It would appear so."

Her face did a funny little twist as she handed

him back the phone. She looked dazed, lost, but also determined.

"We'll talk more after church. For now—" Walker reached out "—let's get inside and find our seats."

Hope accepted his silent invitation, taking his hand without hesitation. But she couldn't prevent a small sob.

"We'll figure it out, Hope."

"I know." Then, just as smoothly as he'd taken her hand, she reached out and grasped one of Kennedy's. Walker took Harper's, and the four of them entered the church linked together hand in hand.

The dream just became a lot more real.

Walker directed their tiny group to one of the back pews. Almost as soon as they were settled, the worship team began playing the first cords of a familiar Christmas hymn.

Proving Hope hadn't neglected their Christian education, Harper and Kennedy launched into the song with enthusiasm. The girls knew most of the words. They mumbled over several of the more difficult phrases, then all but shouted out the chorus, putting solid emphasis on *away* and *manger*.

Walker and Hope shared a smile over the children's heads, the silent message that passed between them seemed to say, "How could anyone not love these two girls?"

The lead pastor took the pulpit. His sermon focused on God's love given to humankind in the gift of His Son. An appropriate message for the season and one Walker considered while the girls silently drew on paper Hope had brought with her.

"We are an active participant in this transaction between God and His people," the preacher continued. "We are to accept this gift that is freely given."

The man's word choice had Walker sitting a little straighter. *We are an active participant.* For years, Walker had remained passive. He'd ignored his blessings in favor of focusing solely on what he'd lost. He'd allowed what might have been to overwhelm what could be.

"Accepting a gift, any gift, starts with a choice."

A choice. Yes, Walker had a choice to make. He could remain stuck in the past where everything was sad yet familiar, or he could reach for an uncertain future full of unknowns. Letting go would not be easy. Rachel's death had shattered his heart. Walker had truly thought he'd buried his one chance at happiness with his wife and daughter.

However, for the first time in years he wanted to try for happily-ever-after again. And it was all due to the woman sitting on his right. The girls had played their role, as well. Walker wanted to be a husband *and* father. He'd quit wanting either. Unable to stop himself, he glanced at Hope over the twins' heads. She was leaning forward, listening intently to the sermon. In a flash, Walker saw what his future held. And whom he wanted to share it with.

Dare he take a leap of faith?

The sermon concluded and the worship band took their place. They played the final song, another Christmas staple. The pastor dismissed the congregation with a prayer and a blessing for the coming week.

Walker and Hope went through the process of swathing the twins in their winter-weather gear. With Hope riding shotgun, and the twins buckled up in the back seat, Walker pointed his SUV toward Quinn's house. When Hope asked why, he simply said, "Tradition."

Her eyes filled with that same look he'd come to recognize as longing. "I thought we were going to buy a Christmas tree."

"After lunch."

Five minutes later, he was pulling his SUV in behind McCoy's beat-up Jeep. He and Hope were helping the girls out of the back seat when Reno's pickup pulled to a stop behind them. "I thought you said this was a *family* tradition."

"Extended family," he corrected. "Which includes lifelong friends, distant cousins and random people any of us want to invite."

"Random people like me." She clearly meant it jokingly, but there was hurt in her tone.

"There is nothing random about you."

Hope gave him a wry smile. Again, Walker wondered about her past, namely her childhood. He wasn't able to ask the question, because Reno hopped out of the truck and stretched his long legs as if working out invisible kinks. His face held signs of pain.

The doctor in Walker frowned at his friend. "You went skiing?"

Reno made a face. "Knock it off, *Mom*. I hit the slopes this morning. Snowboarding, not skiing. And look who it is. Hey, girls. Hope."

"Hi, Reno."

From Walker's point of view, Reno's smile was a little too friendly. As was the one Hope gave him in return. Walker shifted between the two. The move lacked finesse and Reno, hardwired to cut Walker zero slack, made a snarky remark. "Real smooth, man."

Bertha barked a greeting from the porch.

Squealing in delight, the twins took off. Hope shot after them, all but begging them to slow down. A minor commotion ensued at the top of the steps. Then, after a cursory knock on the front door, everyone entered the house.

Walker and Reno pulled up the rear. Reno, incapable of keeping his nose out of anyone's business, wasted no time fishing for information. "What's going on, Walker?"

He pretended to misunderstand. "You and I are about to embark on some serious carbo-loading thanks to my sister's world-famous mashed potatoes."

Reno paused at the foot of the steps, forcing Walker to do the same. "Nice redirect, but something's definitely up. I'm not blind. I see the family connection. Either come clean about those little girls, or I'm going to start drawing conclusions."

"Let it drop, Reno."

"No can do. You're happy again." The other man arrowed a finger in Walker's direction. "And we both know why."

Walker attempted to sidestep his friend and ascend the steps.

Reno moved directly in his path.

"Move out of my way."

"Are Harper and Kennedy your daughters?"

Walker suppressed a ragged sigh. It swelled inside him, hurting like a sip of scalding coffee heading down his windpipe. "No."

Expecting more probing, Reno surprised him with shake of his head. "Too bad. You've been walking around half-dead for way too long. It's been nice seeing you come back to life."

There were a lot of ways Walker could respond to his friend's assessment. He could attempt denial, but why? Reno was right. He'd been moving through life on autopilot for years.

"Yeah, yeah, I get it. Mind my own business." Reno slapped Walker on the back. "Now that I'm through making startling insights, and watching you squirm, I could get down with some serious carbo-loading."

Although he knew this was only a pause in the conversation—Reno was nothing if not persistent—Walker was relieved his friend had let the matter drop for now. "After you."

They entered the house, Reno seeking food, Walker breathless with a different sort of hunger. The kind that couldn't be sated with mashed potatoes. He wanted what Reno accused to be true. He craved a family of his own. Not just any family, either, but the one that could never be his.

He was suddenly aware of the wild beating of his heart.

In silent agreement, he and Reno moved past the entryway, into the living room. An eclectic mix of people had gathered, some sat, others milled about with plates overflowing with food. The majority was family, but a few friends and locals were also in attendance, most of whom

Walker had known since grade school. Some, like Reno, he'd known even longer.

A grin slid across Reno's face. "Lunch is served."

Without another word, his friend took off for the dining room, leaving Walker alone with his thoughts. The exact place he did not want to be. Thankfully, a loud *woof* heralded Bertha's arrival. The massive dog wheeled around the corner, then let out another serious of barks when she eyeballed Walker.

"Hey, big girl." He reached down to pet the dog's head.

"Look what the dog dragged in." Dressed in jeans and a wheat-colored cable-knit sweater, Grant greeted Walker with a grin. "Hope is in the kitchen with my lovely wife."

"Who said I was looking for Hope?"

"Weren't you? My mistake." The man sauntered off chuckling under his breath.

Walker hung back, torn between seeking out Hope or the food. The matter was settled when Reno returned, plate in hand, a snarky look on his face. "You going to stand there petting the dog all day or eat?"

"I'll eat. Thanks, man." He yanked the plate out of Reno's hand and disappeared in the living room to the sound of his friend's outraged sputtering.

* * *

Barely ten minutes after entering the Holloway's home, Hope found herself elbow-deep in flour and cookie dough. This home, these people, they took family to a whole new level. Traditions were as ingrained in their DNA as their hair color. Hope had seen glimpses of the same in her temporary homes, but never before had her mind been able to reach beyond a hazy, unrealized dream and formulate a clear picture of the kind of family she wanted for herself.

Quinn rattled off the recipe's ingredients. Hope was familiar with most, but the last one had her looking up, mystified. "Cardamom?"

"There's something cozy about the spice, don't you think?"

"I have no idea." Hope wasn't even sure what cardamom was.

When she voiced her ignorance, Quinn smiled. "It's a spice from India."

"Did I hear you say cardamom?" Walker appeared in the doorway. "Please tell me you're making my favorite cookies."

Hope angled her head. "Really? They're your favorite?"

"Fastest way to my heart."

His words seemed to have a hidden meaning. Or maybe not so hidden. The moment Walker's gaze locked with hers, Hope thought of family again, of cozy wood and glass houses nestled on a Colorado lake.

For several, painful seconds, her lungs refused to work properly.

Why him, Lord?

Hope knew so little about the man, and certainly nothing about the loss he'd endured that had born that hint of sorrow he wore like a second skin.

The room suddenly felt too small, too hot and crowded. Hope shoved a strand of hair off her face with the top of her wrist. It fell back over her forehead almost immediately. Couldn't her hair at least cooperate, if not her heart?

Walker shifted, splintering the tense moment.

"Stop distracting my helper." Quinn gave him a little shove. "Hope and I have serious work to do."

Walker dug in his heels, making a snide comment about bossy big sisters. Quinn countered with a remark about bratty little brothers. The affection between them was obvious. Hope felt a tug in her heart. She'd seen siblings interact like this. But she'd never really been a part of the good-natured teasing.

Always on the outside looking in. Story of her life. The tug in her heart turned into an ache.

"Go find someone else to bother." Quinn gave Walker another shove.

"All right, all right, but only because the sooner

I leave, the sooner you can get those cookies baked." He gave Hope one long look, then left the kitchen muttering something under his breath she didn't quite catch.

"What was that?" Quinn yelled after him. "Did you just call me a nag?"

His only response was a brief wave over his head.

Hope kept her expression bland as she watched Walker's retreat. She tried to appear nonchalant, easy breezy. But when she realized Quinn was watching her, she was hit with a wall of nerves. Had she just given away her attraction for Walker away? *To his sister?*

Proving she took her role as big sister seriously, Quinn addressed the matter head-on. "What's going on between you and my brother?"

Hope busied herself with picking up the recipe card and pretending avid fascination. "It's not what you think. Walker and I agreed to work together to provide the twins a happy Christmas."

"Admirable, to be sure." Quinn took the recipe card out of Hope's hand. "I'm glad you and Walker have become friends. He needs a friend. He's been alone too long, ever since…"

She let the rest hang in the air. Hope had so many questions. Walker had been alone ever since…what? Would Quinn tell her if she asked?

The woman's continued silence was answer enough. "How many cookies are we making?"

Quinn appeared relieved by the change of subject. "Three batches of thirty-six, one for today, the rest for Grant's office."

"One hundred and eight cookies it is." Hope grabbed the jar of flour, giving Quinn a bland stare before rolling her gaze over the recipe card she still held. "Ready to get back to work?"

The next hour was spent mixing ingredients, rolling out dough, applying cookie cutters and then baking batches of two dozen at a time.

The spicy aroma of cardamom was mouthwatering. "I can't wait to taste these."

"You shall be the first."

Only after the last batch was out of the oven did Hope take Quinn up on her offer. The mix of sugar, butter and cardamom slid over her tongue. "I'm stealing this recipe."

"No need. It's yours."

She'd barely taken a second bite when they were interrupted by two sets of very excited twins. Apparently, sledding was on the afternoon's agenda. "Dad and Uncle Walker are meeting us at the top of the hill," Skylar said.

"Let's sit out on the back porch and watch the shenanigans," Quinn suggested. "Unless you want to join the fun."

"I'm perfectly happy observing."

"I was counting on you saying that."

Outside, Quinn pointed to their left where the sledding party had gathered near a clump of pine trees. The grade of the slope seemed a bit steep for Hope's liking, but it faced away from the lake and leveled out into a flat, snow-covered plain.

Harper and Kennedy bounced around Walker, talking all at once. From this distance, Hope couldn't hear their specific words. She didn't need to know what they said. Their obvious excitement was enough to warm her heart. For his part, Walker looked like—Hope swallowed—he looked like a father as he loaded the twins onto a two-person sled.

He guided them in position, and then...

Whoosh! Down the hill they went. Harper screamed. Kennedy screamed.

Hope jumped to her feet.

She was halfway down the back steps when the shrieks turned to giggles, then to bellyaching laughter. At the bottom of the hill, both girls rolled off the sled, then, hopping to their feet, began jumping up and down and begging to do it again.

Walker ran down the hill, grabbed the sled and trudged back up the slope, the girls scrambling along behind him.

Still shaking a little, Hope returned to her seat next to Quinn and continued watching the fun.

This carefree afternoon with family was the life the twins deserved, and so much more than Hope could provide them.

Had she once thought she could take them back to New York and none of this would matter anymore?

"It's a relief to see Walker happy again. He's shut himself off from the world for so long I'd forgotten how good he is with kids, not just my daughters, but other kids, too."

Hope had a million questions. She settled on, "Has he always worked the night shift?"

"No." Quinn waved at one of her daughters. "He says the hours suit him. But I know it's not true. It's just an excuse to avoid personal connections outside of family."

Too intrigued to let that go, Hope said, "That's the second time you've referenced Walker's past. What aren't you saying?"

"He hasn't told you about Rachel?"

Rachel. Hope now had a name to put to Walker's private pain. There'd been a woman, one that still lived in his heart, if not his life. Hope wanted to retreat inward and isolate herself from the moment. Her curiosity was too strong. "He's never mentioned a Rachel, or any woman for that matter."

"I'm not surprised." Quinn's gaze followed Walker as he loaded the twins onto the sled again.

"Brent isn't the only Evans brother who suffered a terrible loss."

"No?"

"I'm sorry. I've said too much. Walker should be the one to tell you about his wife."

"Walker is married?"

How had her private detective missed that vital piece of information? How had she?

"*Was* married. It was a long time ago."

"What happened?"

Quinn shook her head. "I shouldn't say. If my brother wants you to know what happened, he'll tell you himself."

Hope looked over where Walker stood, laughing with Grant over something one of the little girls said. He seemed genuinely happy. But with Quinn's words rolling around in her head, Hope studied him closer. She noticed how he held himself a little separate. In the moment, and yet not fully there. His loneliness called to her. Hope wanted to go to him and offer what comfort she could. She wanted to listen to his story, maybe soothe away his pain. She wanted to provide him with new memories to chase away the bad ones.

Did she have that right?

"You like him."

Hope gave a weighty sigh. "Of course I like him. He's a friend. I like *all* my friends."

Quinn's lips curved upward. "No man looks at a friend the way my brother looks at you."

Hope shut her eyes. There was no excuse for feeling moved by Quinn's observation. "If Walker considered me more than a friend, he would have told me about his past."

That, Hope realized, was the critical detail she must not forget. She'd put Plan B in motion to secure her future with the twins, not Walker.

"Hope, is it really out of the realm of possibility that you and Walker could be more than friends? Have you considered—"

The man himself interrupted. "We have hungry kids out here. Cookies ready yet?"

Quinn gave him a thumbs-up.

A commotion ensued as adults and children took a break from the sledding. The twins were digging into their first cookie when Kennedy swung a perfectly innocent gaze up to Hope. "Have you thought any more about getting us a puppy?"

Nothing like putting her on the spot.

"You really should take a look," Walker said.

Hope was shaking her head before he finished. "I don't want to see puppies."

"And yet your face says you absolutely do."

"I absolutely do not." She sighed. "I'll just fall in love."

Walker held out a hand. "Come on. You can

take a quick look. Five minutes, and that'll be that."

Hope grappled with indecision. "Five minutes, not a second more."

"I'll start a timer." He pointed to his sports watch, then stopped the twins with another point when they scrambled out of their seats. "You cannot come with us."

Identical scowls formed between their brows. "Why not?"

"Because you'll start begging your aunt for a puppy—" he lowered his voice to a stage whisper "—and then she'll say no for sure."

With their faces full of little-girl mutiny, they relented.

At the top of the basement stairs, Hope hesitated. "Before we head down, I need to know whose side you're on, mine or the twins?"

He gave her a wounded expression. "Must you ask?"

"Actually, yes. Am I about to be manipulated into adopting a puppy?"

"Honestly?" His grin flashed. "Only if you really, really, really want one."

Bracing herself, Hope descended into the basement. Daisy lay peacefully in the basket with her puppies. Four were feeding, but the other three were engaged in a raucous play session.

"They're so cute." Hope lowered to her knees,

her eyes filling with tears as she took in the miniature round, tawny bodies, squat legs, black ears and smashed-in snouts. "I can hardly stand it."

A daring puppy belly-crawled to the edge of the basket. He wiggled over the top and tumbled onto the floor. After a seriously cute dance to gain his feet, he found his balance and shot across the basement at lightning speed. He came to a dead stop, then spun in a circle and sped back in the direction of his siblings. This time his bubblegum-pink tongue flapped out the side of his mouth.

Before Hope could reach for him, the puppy took a flying leap in the air. With momentum on his side, he cleared the edge of the basket and landed on top of the other puppies with a belly splat. He wiggled around, chomping and nipping at random paws, floppy ears and nub tails. Hope stared in momentary shock then, shaking her head, burst out laughing.

With Walker's accompanying chuckle filling the room, she scooped up the troublemaker. He came up wriggling and twisting, little legs running in the air. "Rambunctious little guy, aren't you?"

He continued his antics, sufficiently getting in several licks across her chin. Laughing despite the impromptu bath, she held on tight and studied the animal through narrowed eyes. "You are breaking my heart."

When he stopped thrashing, Hope put him on the floor. He spun around, caught sight of his mother and immediately instigated a wrestling match with her. The good-natured Daisy obliged her rabble-rousing offspring.

"Time's up." Walker stretched out his hand. "It's been five minutes. Ready to go?"

Hope wasn't ready to leave. "One more minute."

"I'll give you two."

She took ten.

Then, heart heavy, she ascended the basement steps in silence. Walker brought up the rear. Upstairs, he took her hand, pulled her close enough she could feel the heat coming off him in waves. "Why so sad?"

She shrugged.

"Talk to me, Hope." He drew her a step closer, so close she could smell the remaining hints of his shampoo—a masculine, spicy scent that brought to mind a forest of fresh pine trees covered under a blanket of snow. They were nearly touching now.

She drew in a shaky breath.

"You were smiling and laughing down there, kissing puppies and letting them kiss you back."

He angled his head. "Now you look like you want to cry. Tell me what's wrong."

Hope said nothing as he guided her to the kitchen table, now empty but for abandoned plates full of cookie crumbs.

Without really thinking about what she was doing, she sat.

Walker took the chair beside her.

"Did you have a dog as a child?" he asked. "I'm shooting in the dark here, but…did he get hit by a car or something?"

"I never had a dog. I always wanted one. But it was out of the question." She looked down at the distressed farm table, dragging her thumbnail along a jagged scar. "Charity and I were shuttled from home to home, some large and full of other kids, some smaller. A few older couples took us in, all of them doing their Christian duty, taking care of the widowed pastor's daughters, 'the poor little dears.'"

Hope hated the bitterness she heard in her tone. She rarely talked about her childhood for this very reason.

"Where was your mother?"

"She died when Charity and I were a few years older than the girls."

"And your father? He was a pastor?"

She nodded. "After my mother died, he became a missionary, working in various undisclosed regions of the world, probably the Middle East, maybe China, but always somewhere dangerous. He came home occasionally, then off he would go again. The church rallied behind him, financially supporting his work and taking turns caring for Charity and me."

"So, your father basically abandoned you and your sister."

She shrugged.

"At least you had each other."

If only it were that simple. "Charity and I weren't close like Harper and Kennedy. We never had that twin connection. We were wired differently. Charity considered every move to a new home as a wild adventure. I dreaded having to start all over again. Holidays were the worst."

"Because of your father's absence?"

Hope didn't want Walker rooting around in her head and making himself at home. *Too late.* She'd already let him in. "He served people living in the worst of conditions. It changed his perspective. He considered America far too indulgent. He disliked Christmas most of all. We were not to celebrate or accept presents. We were to contemplate the plight of others less fortunate."

"That's a lot to ask of children."

"It was especially difficult when we were living with families that had other kids our age."

"Because those kids accepted the full Christmas experience as just a part of their normal existence?"

"Exactly."

"What about other holidays, birthdays? Were those off-limits, as well?"

"They were treated the same as Christmas." She closed her eyes, trying not to remember the shame of wanting something special from her father, nothing big, just something tangible she could hold on to when he left her in the care of strangers. "I don't want that for Harper and Kennedy. I want them to love Christmas. Not because of the presents, my father had a point about that, but about the celebration of family. I want them to know the joy of the season. The food, the baking, the decorations."

"Your sister didn't give them those kinds of Christmases?"

"I'm not sure. I don't think she had the money, or even the inclination." Hope sighed. "It's hard to know. I've asked the twins about their life with their mother. But they only know what they know. What seems normal to them isn't normal for other children."

In a stilted tone, she told him about their request to stay in the car while she went into the hospital to confront him. As he listened, Walker's expression mirrored the concern swirling inside

Hope. "I fear my sister may not have been the most conventional of mothers."

A long pause met her confession. Then, with the insight she was coming to understand as part of who he was as a doctor and as a man, he said, "You're afraid she was abusive?"

"No! Charity made mistakes, but she loved her daughters. It's just… I worry she neglected them."

"Let me ease your mind. I've treated hundreds of children in my ER. Part of what I have to do is to look for signs of abuse. Harper and Kennedy show no signs of it. Yes, they're more reserved than most five-year-old children, and they can be clingy when they're tired or thrown into new situations, but they know they're safe and loved. They're going to be fine."

"That's pretty much what Dr. Stephens said."

Walker considered her with a thoughtful expression. "You've taken excellent care of them, Hope. Never doubt that."

But she did, all the time. "I can't give them everything they need. Although I've tried, I can't be both mother and father to them. And I can't give them a family Christmas, not without your help."

He smiled then. And the look in his eyes—*that look*—was full of unspoken promises. "We're going to give Harper and Kennedy the best

Christmas of their lives. Actually, we've already begun."

She supposed they had.

"And you, Hope." He touched her sleeve, nothing but a slide of his fingertips, but she felt the contact all the way to her toes. "You deserve to experience the joy of a family Christmas as much as the twins. Let me give that to you."

She wanted to believe this time would be different. "I'm not family."

"Now see, that's where you're wrong." He pulled her close and kissed the top of her head. "You are family."

Oh, Walker.

"Now, let's round up the twins and go buy us a Christmas tree." He stood and reached for her. "You with me, Jeffries?"

With fingers shaking slightly, she placed her hand in his. "I'm with you, Evans."

Chapter Thirteen

Walker and Hope found the twins in the living room. They were listening, eyes wide, as McCoy gave his opinion on what kind of tree they should choose. According to his brother, the tree should be at least seven feet tall, a Colorado blue spruce and the only place to find it was Coach's Christmas Tree Lot.

Aware his brother could go on for another thirty minutes, Walker interrupted the one-sided discussion. "Who's ready to pick out our Christmas tree?"

Harper and Kennedy answered immediately. "Me!"

Goodbyes were said. Then, after loading Hope and the twins in his SUV, Walker set out in the direction of Coach's Christmas Tree Lot. He pulled into an empty parking space next to the hand-painted sign announcing he'd found the right place.

As they climbed out of the vehicle, Harper informed their group, "We have to get a Colorado blue spruce. Or nothing at all."

Walker met Hope's amused gaze over the little girl's head. "I'm told this particular lot has a wide variety of blue spruces."

"They have to be *Colorado* blue spruces."

Walker gave the child a fist bump. "Got it."

With the help of one of the coaches, they found the perfect tree. A Colorado blue spruce that was just over seven feet tall with full branches, a straight trunk and no bald spots.

"For an additional ten dollars," the man informed them, "we'll deliver the tree to your house within the next twenty-four hours."

"Thanks, but I think we can manage it ourselves."

It was past dusk, the sky more purple than gray, when Walker drove into his driveway.

By mutual agreement, Hope occupied the twins so he could wrestle the tree off the roof of his SUV and secure a stand to the trunk. When he brought the tree inside the house, he was pleased to discover Hope and the twins had prepared the perfect spot in the living room.

After setting the tree in the now empty space overlooking the lake, he moved it around until Hope was satisfied with its position. "There," she declared. "Right there. Perfect."

Walker removed his gloves and studied the overall effect. "We made a good choice."

He caught Hope's smile, found his own widening in response. This moment with her and the twins felt good. It felt right. No guilt, no looking back, just a full heart and a lot of joy.

Something was churning inside him, something directly related to the smiling woman standing beside him. Each moment in her company was becoming more and more precious. The twins added the exclamation point to every encounter.

Walker's house felt like a home now. The tree wasn't the only reason.

Anticipation sang in his veins, and then…

Ah, yes, there was the pang of familiar guilt he'd been expecting. Tonight, however, the pain that always accompanied the sensation was decidedly less. Time and distance had softened the rough edges of his grief. And now, Walker was ready to admit he had feelings for Hope. She made him want to start living again.

Why not start now?

"Okay, girls, now for the important question. Do we go with white lights or multicolored? No, wait." He held up a hand to stop the twins from shouting out their preferences. "Think very hard before you respond. There is only one right answer."

Both girls turned to Hope. Kennedy spoke for the pair. "Can we show him what we got?"

"Now is as good a time as any." Hope smiled. "Be right back."

With her expression giving nothing away, she disappeared into the kitchen. When she returned, she carried an armful of plastic bags from the big-box store on the edge of town. With a flourish, she dug inside one of the larger bags, then pulled out a box of lights.

Walker's gaze landed on the picture of a Christmas tree aglow with every color in the rainbow. "Now that's what I'm talking about."

Harper rummaged through the other bags. Kennedy, sweet girl that she was, only had eyes for him. "Are you going to stay and help us decorate the tree?"

The question should have thrown him off balance. Walker hadn't decorated a tree since Rachel's death. He waited for images from the past to encroach on the moment. They didn't come. Instead, a very clear picture of Christmas morning swam in his mind. The twins were in flannel nightgowns, sitting among discarded wrapping paper and way too many presents. Walker and Hope drank coffee and watched them tearing into yet another gift.

He was so caught up in the image, he hadn't realized Kennedy was still talking to him.

"Here." She shoved a box of shiny red ornaments into his hands, her eyes full of little-girl excitement. "You can put these on the tree."

Walker automatically closed his fingers over the box. "Ho-kay."

The next two hours went by in a whirlwind of decorating and giggling—on the twins' part—and organized chaos. When the last ornament was hung, Walker stepped back and studied their collective handiwork.

"It doesn't look right," Harper complained.

"That's because the little lights aren't twinkling." He turned to Hope. "Want to do the honors?"

"You better believe I do." Looking happier than he'd seen her all day, she trotted to the wall socket and plugged in two sets of cords.

An explosion of color erupted from every available branch.

"Best tree ever," Walker declared, earning him a pair of matching fist bumps from the twins.

Hope returned to his side then, stunning him speechless, she linked her arm through his and laid her head on his shoulder. "We make a great team."

"We do."

She lifted her head.

Their gazes locked, held. Walker couldn't look away. Hope seemed caught with the same affliction. The twins settled in on either side of them, gazing up at the tree with wonder.

Walker's heart filled with a flourish of warmth and long-missed happiness. In that moment, the future seemed as bright as the multicolored Christmas tree.

Both girls were practically asleep in their chairs by the time Hope served dinner, a simple meal of pasta and a green salad. They'd been able to convince Walker to stay for the meal. Hope watched him out of the corner of her eye, an uneasy sensation making her shoulders bunch.

Something had changed in the last few minutes. Over dinner, they'd fallen into an easy conversation about random topics from the weather to Walker's plan for decorating the outside of his house. "I'll get it done this week."

"Tell me what I can do to help."

"I'll send a long, extensive list."

They shared a laugh. And everything seemed right in the world. However, now, beneath the girls' sleepy chatter boiled unspoken tension. Hope thought they'd gotten on well today and were beginning to trust each other. But she'd caught Walker watching her from across the table, his brows knit together, as if he had yet to determine if she was his enemy or his ally.

She wasn't sure herself. Which probably explained the strain.

Needing to alleviate a portion of the awkwardness, she smiled at him. He smiled back.

"It was a great day," she said.

"The very best."

Yawning loudly, Harper rubbed her eyes. "Will you read to us tonight, Aunt Hope?"

The question sent warmth washing through her. She and the girls may be staying in an unfamiliar town, in an unfamiliar house, but Hope could—and would—continue reading to the girls at night. Dr. Stephens had emphasized the importance of routine. All Hope knew was that the bedtime ritual was as important to her as it seemed to be for the girls.

She realized she hadn't answered the question when Kennedy chimed in. "Will you join us, Dr. Walker?"

Hope didn't want Walker invading her special time with the twins. But the silent plea in the little girls' eyes nearly wrecked her. How was she supposed to say no to that look? She locked eyes with Walker. The longing in them made her decision for her. "Do you want to come upstairs and read to the girls with me?"

He lifted a shoulder, trying to look nonchalant. Hope wasn't fooled. He wanted to join them. "What are you reading?"

"The Night Before Christmas."

"My favorite."

The four of them trooped out of the kitchen, the girls dragging at an impossibly slow pace that spoke of their exhaustion. Hope figured they wouldn't make it past the first page.

At the last minute, Walker turned back in the direction of the kitchen. "It's trash day tomorrow. I better take the can to the edge of the drive before I forget."

She nodded, then he did, and they went their separate ways.

By the time the twins were tucked into the queen-size bed in one of the upstairs bedrooms, their faces washed, teeth brushed and prayers said, Hope's heart had taken a series of hits. The twins had prayed for her, for their mother in heaven, then had added several more for Walker, Quinn, the Holloway twins, McCoy. They'd finished with Bertha and Daisy.

Then Harper had added, "Please, Lord. Make Aunt Hope change her mind so we can get one of Daisy's puppies."

Kennedy had her own final request. "Can you make it so we can stay in Colorado forever and ever? And can you make Skylar and Sinclair our best friends? Dr. Walker, too? We like him a lot."

"A lot, a lot," Harper added.

The girls had opened their eyes, grinned at

each other, then said, in unison, with one solid nod in agreement, "Amen."

Eyes stinging, heart shattered into a million pieces, Hope accepted the truth. Harper and Kennedy were already thinking of themselves as a part of the Evans family. Or certainly wanting it to be true. They would be thrilled when they discovered the truth.

She sat in a chair next to the big bed they shared, opened the book in her lap and looked over at the twins.

Two pair of big blue eyes stared back at her. They had something on their minds.

"Girls? What's up?"

They looked at one another, exchanged one of their silent twin messages, then turned back to study Hope with identical expressions of wistfulness.

"Do you like Dr. Walker?" Harper asked.

Hope knew where this was going. She'd assumed the twins had let this particular topic go. "Of course I like him. I think he's nice."

"Do you think you could marry him?" the child asked. "And then you could be our mommy and he could be our daddy and we can live in this house forever and ever."

Hope sighed over the vulnerable expression in the young girl's eyes. "Dr. Walker can't be your daddy."

"But you said you liked him," Harper whined. "And when Momma said she liked a man, he would move in with us."

Oh, Charity. A keen ache pierced the center of Hope's soul.

She was going to have to tell the twins about Brent if he didn't arrive in the next few days. In the meantime, she sidestepped the issue of fathers altogether by saying, "It's best Dr. Walker and I stay friends for now."

For now? Why had Hope added that qualifier? *You know why.*

And so, apparently, did the twins. They exchanged another look. Hope feared two little matchmakers had been born tonight. Praying she was wrong, she lowered her head and started reading. "'Twas the night before Christmas and all through the house…"

Walker stood outside the twins' bedroom, listening as Hope's soft, lilting voice read the popular Christmas story. Her voice was filled with an underlying tenderness, as if she was feeling especially emotional tonight.

Unwilling to interrupt the tender moment, he peered into the room. His gaze sought and found Hope. Head bent, there was a softness about her that sent his head reeling. He had to look away to catch his breath.

Walker tried not to read too much into his reaction. Hope was reading to his nieces. His nieces! The knowledge was still new, making him as emotional as she sounded. The three were living in his home, as if they were family.

They were family.

Just not *his* family.

Hope paused, looked up and caught him staring. She kept reading from memory, her green eyes searching his as she spoke. Her gaze was full of profound gentleness, as if she shared the conflict waging inside him. He wanted to go to her, let her soothe away whatever this was moving through him.

She mercifully looked back to the book.

On surprisingly unsteady legs, Walker quietly slipped down the hallway. He left the house through the back door and sat heavily on the stoop. He drew in a deep breath, let it out slowly and then stared up at the clouds skidding across the full moon.

He attempted to picture Rachel in his mind. She came to him, the image clearer than in recent years. He breathed in. Out. And then…he let his wife go.

Peace enveloped him.

The process had been so simple. Why hadn't he done this sooner?

Because Hope hadn't come into his life, mak-

ing him wish for something more than a bland
existence and terrible work hours. She'd awak-
ened a desire to start living again, without grief
weighing him down.

What if she left Colorado?

What if she didn't?

Working the question around in his mind, he
stared out over the lake and watched the moon-
light shimmer across the water.

Behind him, the door creaked on its hinges.
"Walker?"

"Out here," he called over his shoulder. "On
the back stoop."

Hope poked her head out the doorway. "I
thought you'd left."

"Not yet." Without thinking too hard about
what he was doing, he patted the spot beside him.
"Come. Sit with me a moment before I head out."

"Let me get my coat."

She returned in less than a minute and sat.

Walker could feel her eyes on him. She had to
be wondering why he hadn't come into the room
to read with the twins as he'd promised.

He wasn't sure how to explain it.

Gathering his thoughts, he looked up at the sky.

As if sensing he had something important to
say, she reached out and covered his hand with
hers. The tension drained out of him and he knew

where to start. "I like having you and the twins in my house."

"Thank you for inviting us."

"It made sense." He swiveled his head in her direction and decided to be candid. "I heard your conversation with the twins tonight."

"Which part?"

Rather than rehashing the conversation, he said, "It's not a bad idea, you and me."

"It's a terrible idea." He would have been insulted if not for the tender expression in her eyes, and the yearning. "They think if we got married, you would become their father. You can't be their father."

She was right, of course. Brent had that honor. The reminder felt like another loss.

"Even if your brother denies paternity, or fails to—"

"He won't."

"Then there's nothing more to say."

Oh, but there was. "There's something between us, Hope." He took her hand in his. "I know you feel it, too."

"We barely know each other."

"We know enough."

"You may know enough about me. But I know very little about you."

"That's not completely true."

"No?" She turned her face away from his.

"What about your wife? Were you ever going to tell me about Rachel?"

Not expecting that, Walker stared out at the lake. He traced the moon's path across the water, gathered his words. "How much did your investigator tell you about Rachel?"

"Nothing, actually. It was Quinn."

Quinn, of course.

Dragging in a ragged breath, he turned to face Hope. "Did my sister tell you Rachel was five months pregnant when she died?"

His voice sounded as empty as he felt.

"Oh, Walker. No." Tears filled her eyes. "I... I didn't know. I'm so sorry."

He rose, unable to sit still, and paced a few steps toward the lake. He stopped and shoved his hands in his pockets. "Rachel had just reached the halfway mark in her pregnancy, about nineteen and a half weeks along, when the pain began."

"She was losing the baby?"

"That's what we both thought. What we didn't know was that her appendix had ruptured. By the time the doctors realized the problem, it was too late. The toxins had already moved into her blood. The baby survived in the NICU for a few days after Rachel died, but..."

The rest of his words floated over the lake.

"Oh, Walker." Hope moved to stand beside him. "I'm sorry."

They shared a sad smile. He looked down at his open palm and dusted it with the other. He'd never confided so much to anyone outside the family, and certainly not to a woman. But now that he'd begun, he needed to tell Hope the rest, the part that came after Rachel's death. "I didn't allow myself to grieve. It felt too… I don't know, indulgent. I turned to work to numb my pain and have been living that way ever since."

He shut his eyes a moment, tried to bring up one last image of Rachel. But the reality of Hope was too strong. Her lovely, oval face, the gentle, bowed lips and green eyes, their color so unique they seemed to contain hints of some undiscovered shade. His mind filled with her. How could a woman so deserving of love have received so little? Walker wanted to give her the love she deserved.

The Lord had blessed him with a second chance at happiness. He forced opened his eyes and focused solely on Hope. He swallowed.

She did the same.

"I was happy enough going through the motions, moving from one day to the next, but not really living. Then you and the twins strolled into my ER and everything changed."

She blinked, but didn't say anything.

"Tonight, in my living room," he said. "You, me, the twins, we were a family."

"But, Walker." A sob sounded in her throat. "We can't be a family. Brent is the twins' father. We have to tell them."

Something hot and miserable moved through Walker. "I'm not convinced we should. Brent will be home in a few days. The news should come from him."

She looked so panicked, so defeated, Walker forgot all about his own pain and dragged her into his arms. For a moment, they simply stood wrapped in each other's embrace.

"Hope." He spoke her name with as much gentleness as he could. "Even if we don't tell them about their father, they should at least know they belong to the Evans family."

She stepped out of his arms. "What if they react badly?"

"Do you honestly believe they'll find the news upsetting?"

"No." She sighed. "They'll be thrilled."

Knowing how hard that was for her to admit, Walker pulled her back into his arms and received the shock of his life. It was him that was immediately soothed. Him that felt the rightness of them being together.

"Walker?" Hope whispered his name, encouraging him to tap into the part of his nature he'd buried with Rachel. "I don't know how I'll bear losing them. I… I don't want to be alone anymore."

"You're not alone," he whispered into her hair. "You have me."

She shifted in his arms and looked into his eyes. He saw the truth gazing back at him. She wanted what he wanted, but she was afraid to believe it was real.

He had those same fears.

A severe sensation took over his body and he felt the blood rush through his veins. Her silent call was too strong to ignore. He lowered his head, stopped when his mouth was mere inches from hers. "Tell me to step back. Tell me to let you go. Tell me you don't want me to kiss you."

Her answer was to slip her hands around his neck. It was all the encouragement he needed. His mouth moved over hers.

She sighed into him.

The sound brought him to his senses. Things were moving too fast, for both of them. He abruptly let her go.

A shaken breath escaped her.

"Hope…" He was talking to her back.

Walker didn't follow her inside the house. They both needed time to sort through their feelings. And then? *Then* they would discuss the future.

Chapter Fourteen

Hope woke the next morning to clear skies and an unmistakable reality. She'd lost her heart to Walker Evans. This wasn't supposed to have happened. She'd come to Thunder Ridge to confront the twins' father, obtain his signature on the custody papers, then return to New York with her future set.

Nothing had gone according to plan.

Hope had been naive when she and the twins had boarded the plane in New York. Now, she felt lost, unmoored. She didn't know what came next, or where to turn. Her gaze fell on the Bible she kept by the bedside. Couldn't hurt. She opened to 2 Corinthians and contemplated the highlighted section in the twelfth chapter.

My grace is sufficient for thee: for My strength is made perfect in weakness.

She wasn't alone. She had the Lord. And, according to the man himself, she had Walker. Her feelings for him were growing every day. What they shared seemed real, but Hope wasn't sure if the twins formed the glue that bound them together, or if it was something more.

They needed time, which they would get now that she'd put Plan B into motion. Of course, nothing could be decided until Brent came home. Everything hinged on his arrival.

Putting the future out of her mind, Hope helped the twins dress for the day. In the kitchen, she pulled out the ingredients for their breakfast. As her hands scrambled eggs, her mind went back to Walker. Hard not to think of him when she was living in his home. If Brent didn't step up as the twins' father, could she and Walker make a home for them here? The thought brought such anticipation, she had to take in a few slow breaths.

Kennedy chose that moment to come running into the kitchen, her little face scrunched up in a picture of concern. "Christmas is next week."

"You are correct."

"But we haven't bought any presents for Dr. Walker or Miss Quinn or the twins or the puppies or for, well, anybody."

This, Hope decided, was an easy enough problem to fix. "We'll go shopping after breakfast."

Thirty minutes later, she was parking her rental

car outside The Slippery Slope. "We'll buy something for Dr. Walker first."

The idea was met with excited approval.

She escorted the twins inside the shop and looked around for Reno. Surely, he would know what they should buy his friend. A salesclerk with a mouthful of braces told them the owner wasn't in yet, but she'd be happy to help them. "We're looking for a Christmas gift for a man who likes to ski."

"Does he prefer skiing, or snowboarding?"

Hope felt a moment of sheer panic. How could she have fallen for the man when she didn't even know whether he preferred skiing over snowboarding? "Maybe we should go with something simple, like gloves."

"I can work with that." The clerk led them to a table filled with a wide variety, including mittens, which according to the teenager kept your fingers warmer than gloves during a long day on the slopes. Hope figured someone living in Colorado would know this.

"There are so many choices," Kennedy breathed.

That was an understatement.

It took less than two minutes for Hope to realize she'd made a bad decision. The twins couldn't decide on color or style or whether they should go with gloves or mittens.

"Let's see if I can help." The salesgirl asked

a few questions, then began pulling out several options.

The girls agonized over their selection. "It has to be just the right pair," Harper declared.

Eventually, they narrowed the decision down to two possibilities. When they couldn't come to a consensus, Hope stepped in. "Why don't we get both?"

The clerk offered to get two boxes, which were in the back. While she was gone, they wandered around the store. In the kids' section, her eyes landed on tiny snowboards and miniature skis. Would Walker teach them? Or would their father?

One thing was for certain, it wouldn't be Hope. Needing to distract herself, she asked the girls, "Have you thought about what you want for Christmas?"

"We think about it all the time." Harper's eyes settled on her with a clarity that gave her a bad feeling in the pit of his stomach. "We want a daddy of our very own."

"And we want it to be Dr. Walker," Kennedy added.

"We talked about this already," she croaked out. "Dr. Walker is—"

Kennedy cut her off. "—the daddy we want."

Harper agreed with a vigorous nod.

The wistful look both girls sent Hope shot past every argument she could come up with, except one. The twins already had a father who was currently traveling across the globe to meet them. She wished Walker was with them. He always seemed to know what to say.

"Let's think of other items to add to your Christmas list," she said carefully, attempting to diffuse the situation with a bit of old-fashioned distraction. "In case other people in town want to know what to get you."

"If we can't have a daddy," Harper said, eyes flashing, "then we want a puppy."

Hope nearly agreed to the request. For all the wrong reasons. "I'm still thinking about that, but it's a definite maybe."

The two turned their backs on Hope, then huddled together over a bin of beanie toys. They were subdued the rest of the day. Later that night, once the girls were asleep, Hope lay in own bed, staring up at the ceiling. The twins had asked her about Dr. Walker during bath time, then again after prayers. Hope had told them he was working at the hospital, which seemed to appease them. For now.

It wouldn't last long. The twins were already too attached to Walker. They needed to understand why he couldn't be their father. Knowing it was time to tell them the truth, she picked up her cell phone and composed a text. Any news from Brent?

Walker's response came a few minutes later. Just another update to tell me he's still en route.

Hope blew out a frustrated breath. The girls are asking questions. It's time we tell them about Brent.

Heart pounding, she watched the floating bubbles on the phone's screen. Walker's answer was heroically neutral. I'll come by first thing in the morning after my shift. We'll tell them together.

Hope sent a thumbs-up emoji, then set aside her phone.

There was nothing left to do but mourn what might have been had Walker been the twins' father instead of Brent.

Walker was still thinking about Hope's text as his shift wound down. The last time they spoke, she'd seemed okay letting Brent tell the twins he was their father. Something had changed her mind, and Walker had a good idea what as he reread her text. The girls are asking questions. It's time we tell them about Brent.

Translation: the twins were asking for a father. Had Walker's name come up again? The yearning that came with the thought was a physical ache in his chest. He was ready to join the living again. No more pretending the overnight hours suited his biological clock. No more burying himself in work so he could avoid personal connections.

His awakening didn't mean he would forget Rachel. She would always hold a special place in his heart. But she was his past.

Hope was his future.

The tricky part would be convincing her of that.

Not bothering to change out of his scrubs, he grabbed his gear. Before he could head out, one of the ER nurses peeked her head over the top of his cubicle. "Dr. Evans, you have a visitor. He's waiting for you in the employee break room."

Brent. Who else could it be?

Walker could hear nothing but the sound of his pulse rushing through his veins. Time seemed to crawl. Brent's arrival meant Walker's time with Hope and the twins was over. He'd still see them, but it wouldn't be the same. He tried to shove aside the bitterness that took hold. Tried and failed.

Hope needed to know Brent was home. Walker pulled out his phone. As he typed, he said, "Tell my brother I'll be there in five minutes."

The nurse didn't move. "How did you know it was your brother waiting for you?"

Walker lifted a shoulder. "Lucky guess?"

She left shaking her head.

Alone, Walker texted Hope the news of Brent's unexpected arrival. Almost immediately floating bubbles appeared on the screen. They disappeared for an extended period of time, then came back up. They disappeared again and then—finally—her response came through. Nothing more than a brief Thanks for the heads up and a promise she would have the girls dressed and ready to meet their father.

With leaden steps, Walker made his way to the employee break room. His brother's voice wafted through the open doorway. "You said he'd be here in five minutes." Brent's low-pitched baritone teemed with frustration. "It's been ten. Are you sure he's coming?"

"It's been seven and, yes, he's coming."

Same impatient Brent. Walker shook his head.

Eyes gritty, throat raw with emotion, he stepped into the doorway and confronted his brother's scowl. No doubt his own expression was equally fierce. His suspicion was confirmed when the nurse glanced from one brother to the other, then beat a hasty retreat.

Arms crossed over his chest, eyes narrowed, Brent waited for Walker to enter the room. The calm demeanor was a facade. The man practically hummed with barely controlled energy.

Walker felt a snap of impatience himself.

Clearly, the years of separation hadn't eased the tension between them. And the blame fell firmly on Walker. A sense of inevitability slammed through him. It was time he humbled himself and healed the rift he'd created.

He quickly scanned Brent's face, noticing the dark circles under his eyes and the lines of strain around his mouth. "You look awful."

"Good to see you, too, bro." Brent's lips twisted at a wry angle. "What can I say? Flights out of Africa aren't exactly easy to come by on short notice."

"You were supposed to contact me when you arrived in Germany."

Brent broke eye contact. "Yeah, well, I didn't."

The hostility was nothing new. Again, Walker's fault. He was handling their reunion poorly. Putting his brother on the defense was the exact opposite approach he should be taking. "I'm glad you're home."

Brent's eyebrows slammed together.

Walker recognized that look. *Here it comes.* The pushback, the detailed list of past transgressions, the reminder he'd made a complete mess of their relationship with his lectures and holier-than-thou comparisons.

The fault was his, Walker knew, and he should take the first step toward reconciliation. "I'm sorry, Brent."

"What, exactly, are you sorry for? That I had to beg, borrow and sell half my possessions to get on a flight home? That I had a three-day layover because of bad weather? Or maybe you're sorry because you just can't stop judging me?"

"I'm sorry for all of it. I'm sorry for my lack of understanding after Nicole died. I'm sorry for expecting your experience to be the same as mine, and for spouting off the same tired sermons about it not being too late to change your ways."

"That was certainly a mouthful."

And Walker wasn't finished. "You had every right to grieve Nicole in your own way, as I had the right to grieve Rachel in mine. Who better than me to understand what you were going through? But instead of offering understanding, I lectured and judged you. I was wrong."

Brent gave him an odd look. "You finished?"

"Not quite." He yanked Brent into a ferocious hug. "Welcome home."

Brent returned the hug, added a few slaps on the back, then stepped away and eyed Walker thoughtfully. "You've changed."

"I had help."

Questions lit in the other man's gaze, but he didn't voice them. The restraint was new. As was the apology in his eyes. "You were right to lecture me," Brent admitted. "I was on a bad path. I hurt a lot of people, and all I can do is start making amends, beginning right now. I'm sorry, Walker."

"Don't be too hard on yourself. We both made mistakes, but I know what kind of man you are.

And I know once you meet the twins you'll do the right thing."

"The twins." Brent moved to the window and looked out, his shoulders tense. "You're sure they're my daughters?"

"You'll take a DNA test but, yes, I'm sure. I sent you pictures."

"I've looked at them a million times. They... yeah, I believe they're mine." He took a long, slow inhale of air. Blew it out. "I don't know anything about being a father."

"You aren't in this alone, Brent. We'll help you every step of the way."

Still looking out the window, Brent rocked back on his heels. When he turned back around, his expression was full of suspicion. "We?"

"Me, the family, their aunt."

"The one I spoke with on the phone? Charity's sister."

"That's the one."

Brent didn't look convinced. "The last time we saw each other, you told me I was immature, reckless and irresponsible. That's not a man who should father two little girls."

"I was wrong."

"But that's the thing. You weren't wrong. I was everything you said." Brent ran a hand over his face, drew in another long pull of air. "There are some mistakes a man can never outrun, mistakes that can't be forgiven."

"That's not true. The Lord forgives our transgressions. If you would just turn to Him and—" Walker cut off the rest of his words before he fell into the same old trap of lecturing his brother.

Brent didn't seem to notice his restraint. "The Lord forgives, that's true. But He doesn't always take away the consequences of our sin. You said that to me once, Walker, and you were right. I may never make restitution for my actions, but I'm here to try."

"I didn't say you had to *earn* forgiveness by hopping on a plane to Africa."

"I had one motive when I left the country, and that was to forget what I did."

"You didn't kill Nicole."

Brent's eyes glazed over, as if he was trapped in a horrible memory and couldn't find his way out. "Didn't I?"

"There was an inquiry," Walker reminded him. "The rope's manufacturer was at fault. You were exonerated of any blame."

Walker understood Brent's deep-rooted anger at himself. Until recently, he'd struggled with the same emotion. Brent had been selfish, prideful and determined to live life on his own terms, all because he'd been grieving. Walker, on the other hand, had buried his grief in work.

Neither had found freedom, only a self-made prison of their own making.

"Now that we've covered the past," Brent said, moving away from Walker to pace the room. "Tell me about my—" his steps slowed "—daughters."

Walker did as his brother requested, in great detail. Concluding with, "They're incredibly sweet and beautiful, and you are the most blessed man I know."

"Blessed? I've lost five years of their lives." Brent sounded outraged, a man who'd been wronged by a woman he'd hardly known. He also sounded like a father.

"You really didn't know Charity was pregnant?"

"After we decided to go our separate ways, she cut ties completely." Brent made another pass through the room. "I tried to contact her before I left for Africa. My calls and texts went unanswered. I never knew about the baby. I mean, babies. There are two of them." Wonder filled his voice. "I have *two* daughters."

They grinned at each other, and another layer of hostility fell away.

"When can I meet them?"

Walker moved to the doorway, "How about now?"

Brent joined him on the threshold, paused. "You shouldn't be this easy on me."

"You'd rather I was difficult?"

Sighing, Brent shook his head. "No."

"I need to tell you about Charity's sister," Walker said in a voice as normal as he could. "Hope did the right thing, searching for the twins' father. She didn't have to bring Harper and Kennedy to Thunder Ridge, but she did."

"Your point?"

"The twins love her. She loves them. I won't let you tear them apart."

"You care for her? For Hope?"

"Yes, very much." The truth hit him at last, staggering in its impact.

Walker didn't just care for Hope. He loved her. His feelings were different than the ones he'd had for Rachel, because Hope was different. Walker was, too. And now, he had to trust that God was in control. He had to accept the blessing that had come into his life. "I'm going to ask Hope to stay in Thunder Ridge."

"I see." From the knowing look in his brother's eyes, Walker figured Brent saw the situation pretty accurately.

Walker stepped into the hallway. "Ready to meet your daughters?"

"I've been ready since I learned of their existence."

Chapter Fifteen

Hope waited in the living room for Walker to arrive with his brother. She stared out at the lake without really seeing it. She wasn't sure how long she'd been standing there. A few minutes? Ten? Twenty? She'd lost all concept of time.

Snow fell from the sky in a soft, gentle rhythm, blanketing the lawn in pristine white. The peaceful scene was at odds with the anxiety beating against her ribs. Behind her, the girls strung popcorn and discussed their trip to meet Santa the next day. They agreed they would speak to him together. Harper would sit on Santa's right knee while Kennedy sat on his left.

They plotted what they would ask for from the big guy. A puppy was on the top of their wish list. Apparently, they'd let go of wanting a father. Or so Hope assumed. But when their voices dropped to a whisper, she heard Walker's name, followed by her own.

She glanced over her shoulder. Two identical heads were bent together, conspiring about very important matters. Whatever they were saying to each other, it wasn't meant for her ears.

Probably for the best.

Their father was en route from the hospital, riding shotgun in Walker's SUV. Nothing would ever be the same after he stepped into this room.

Lord, please...

The front door opened and then shut with a soft click. The twins were so involved in their plotting they didn't notice. The sound of masculine voices wafted on the air, and still the girls whispered among themselves.

Walker said something low that made the other man laugh softly. Walker spoke again, his words muffled, but Hope knew it was his voice. Odd that she recognized his rich baritone immediately. They'd only known each other for a few weeks.

The voices grew louder.

Hope turned to face the hallway. No decisions had to be made today.

The voices grew louder, closer, mingling with the heavy, masculine footsteps.

Hope's breath clogged in her throat. The twins looked up.

Now came the moment of truth. No regrets, she told herself.

This is what you want for them.

She forced herself to step back, away from the twins. She'd promised herself she would remain a witness to this first meeting, a bystander.

Always on the outside looking in.

"Dr. Walker's here." The girls hopped to their feet.

Another second passed.

And then…

Walker entered the room, still dressed in scrubs, his jawline tight and peppered with dark stubble.

"Dr. Walker." Harper and Kennedy squealed in delight and rushed to him.

He greeted them with the customary hug and fist bumps. Over their heads, he sought Hope's gaze. Something passed between them, a silent message that her heart understood but her mind refused to comprehend. She was reminded of that first time their eyes met in the ER. Her heart had taken a hit that day. She had never fully recovered.

Another man entered the room, a near carbon copy of his older brother. His movements were full of unmistakable nerves and… Hope's heart dropped to her toes. Brent's gaze was filled with anticipation. He looked at Hope, gave her a short nod, which she returned. And then he smiled directly at the twins.

They started toward him without an ounce of hesitation, as if something in their DNA gravitated to its source.

Hope fell back a step. She hadn't expected that immediate connection.

Walker came to stand beside her. The sorrow in his expression matched her own. *We're in this together.* She felt a little bit less alone.

He took her hand and her restraint nearly shattered. Every bit of moisture dried up in her throat. She'd found a purpose with the twins and could only watch it melt away as Brent Evans lowered to his knees in front of them. "Hi, there. You must be Harper and Kennedy."

Hand in hand, they nodded, drawing closer to him. Closer. Closer.

He began speaking to them in soft tones, commenting on their clothing, their pretty eyes, asking questions about their likes and dislikes, becoming their father with every careful word he spoke.

Hope heard the wonder in his voice. She saw the gleam of fatherly pride swimming in his eyes, and the tears. It was the tears that shattered the last of Hope's doubts. Brent hadn't known about his daughters until Walker's phone call.

That meant Charity had wronged him in one of

the worst possible ways a wife could wrong her husband. Hope felt her knees buckle under the realization that her sister had lied to her. Walker kept hold of her hand, an anchor in the storm of her swirling emotions.

What was she supposed to do now?

Nothing. Hope was supposed to do nothing. Five years ago, Brent Evans and Hope's sister had created two perfect little girls. For years, Charity had kept Brent from knowing his daughters. He deserved to know them.

The twins were equally in awe of the man kneeling in front of them, as if somehow sensing he was theirs.

Feeling mildly desperate, torn between grief and joy, Hope glanced at Walker. He was watching the interaction with watery eyes.

No help there.

At some point, someone would have to tell the girls Brent was their father. But not now.

Kennedy beamed up at him. There was no nervousness in the child, no fear. Just innocent curiosity. "You look like Dr. Walker."

Brent gave the child a warm smile. "That's because I'm his brother."

"Like Aunt Hope was our mom's sister."

He glanced at Hope, giving her a quick once-over. "Sort of like that, yes." His voice was hoarse with emotion. "I'm your…" He swallowed again. "I'm Brent, and I'm your fath—"

He cut off the rest of his words, something preventing him from declaring himself just yet. Perhaps he simply wanted the children's easy manner to continue, or maybe he didn't want to watch their smiles disappear when he declared who he was and why he hadn't come to them sooner.

"Do you have a dog?" Kennedy asked him.

"No, but I want one."

"Daisy had puppies. You want to see them?"

He ran his gaze around the room, landing on Walker. "You got a dog?"

Kennedy giggled. "No, silly. Daisy is Miss Quinn's dog. You should take us over to look at the puppies."

"Can we go over there now, Aunt Hope?" Harper asked. "Can we?"

Brent glanced over to Hope, rose to his full height and studied her a few seconds longer. "You look just like her."

"We were identical twins."

"I see it now. I know it's been a rough few months, and you didn't have to search for me, so…" He paused, his eyes held hers for a few beats. "Thank you."

Two words, that's all it took, and Hope knew she would relinquish the girls without a battle. Eventually. Not yet, though. There were too many details to work out. Legalities to sort through. All of this, assuming Brent wanted to be a full-time father.

He could decide to return to Africa.

Hope didn't want him to do that. She didn't want the twins to have to suffer the same childhood she had.

As if reading her mind, he said, "I'm home for good."

She didn't know whether to laugh or cry.

"You have questions?"

"Several."

His gaze dropped to where her hand was joined with Walker's. Looking as if he had a few questions of his own, he said, "We'll talk later. Right now, I have a litter of puppies to admire. Do you want to come with us?"

She glanced at the twins, both of whom seemed to have forgotten she was in the room. They were too busy gazing up at their father with adoration.

"I'll follow along in a few minutes."

"Good enough."

Hand still clutching Walker's, Hope watched the three leave the house. The door closed with a sharp snap. And that, she realized, was the end. She'd lost the twins to their father.

Tears welled in her eyes. In that moment, Hope didn't think she could feel any more destitute. She was wrong. Walker released her hand, and it was as if the entire world had turned against her. What was she supposed to do next?

Protect the twins.

Protect them against what? A happy childhood with a loving father who came with aunts, uncles and cousins. And, oh yeah, puppies.

The tears fell then.

Walker drew her into his arms. "This is a good thing, Hope."

His voice held as much raw emotion as she felt. "I know."

"You could still fight him for custody."

She could. "That would only end up hurting the twins."

He continued holding her, rubbing her back, whispering words of comfort she desperately needed. Tossing aside her pride, she clung to him. "You will always be their aunt."

It had to be enough.

Conversations would have to occur in the next few days, dozens of them, but the most important question had been answered. Brent was going to step up.

"He won't cut you out of their lives." Walker set her away from him and stared into her eyes. "I won't let him."

The situation was unbearable, and this man's kindness was only making the pain harder to bear. She lowered her head.

"Hey, look at me." He applied gentle pressure under her chin until she did as he requested. "No decisions have to be made today."

She'd had the same thought, but the sooner the future was settled, the better for the twins. "I thought we were going to be a family."

"Me, too."

They'd never said the words aloud until this moment. They hadn't needed to say them. It had been understood.

"It hurts to discover we were wrong."

She nodded.

"I'm sorry, Hope. So very sorry for us both." He gave her lips a gentle kiss, the kind that was meant to soothe. Hope thought her heart might shatter in her chest.

"Christmas Eve is only a few days away." He kissed her temple, lingered there a moment. "Let's focus on enjoying the rest of the holidays."

What was the point? They would basically be putting off the inevitable. But Hope wanted this time with Walker and his family. She wanted it for the twins.

She wanted it for herself.

Chin up, eyes moist, she produced a smile that came at great cost. "I guess all that's left is to go admire Daisy's puppies."

He pressed his forehead to hers. "That's the spirit."

* * *

Later that night, Hope sat at the kitchen table in Walker's house. He'd positioned himself on her right. Brent had chosen the chair directly across from her. The girls were sleeping in their beds. Puppies, new friends and the excitement about meeting Santa the next day had worn them out.

Brent looked equally beat, but there was an underlying joy in him that showed past the exhaustion. He was already in love with his daughters.

Snow fell outside the bay window, obscuring the view of the lake. The lazy, floating flakes seemed in no hurry to find a resting place. Hope felt a little like that, as if she was drifting along without a purpose.

All that was left was a series of conversations. She opened the discussion with a brief history of the twins' lives since they'd shown up on her doorstep. Walker stayed silent throughout the story, letting her explain the situation in her own way. "The girls have had a lot of upheaval in the past eight months."

This seemed to be the opening Brent had been waiting for since sitting down. "Let me take this moment to thank you for taking such good care of them."

"They're family," she said simply. "Family is everything."

"True." The look he shot Walker was full of

apology. Hope was happy to see the brothers making inroads toward healing their relationship, something she was never fully able to do with Charity. And now she was sad.

"I was sorry to hear about Charity's death. She was a vibrant, passionate woman. Truly special."

Hope swallowed back a sob. How could he be this kind about a woman who'd lied and cheated him out of five years with his daughters?

"I also want to thank you for seeking me out," Brent continued. "The girls, my daughters…" He paused, choked on a breath, then began again. "My daughters are amazing little girls, beautiful on the inside and out, and I can't believe I've missed five years of their lives. I won't miss another day, that much I promise you."

He was saying all the right things. No, not just saying them. Meaning them. Hope heard the sincerity in his voice. "I believe you."

"I can't begin to repay you for the gift you've given me."

"I didn't bring the girls to Thunder Ridge for you, Brent. I did it for them."

"Understood. But it must have been difficult coming here."

Like ripping her heart out of her chest. "It was the right thing to do."

Silence fell over the table, all three lost in their own thoughts.

Hope started to speak, but Brent had more to say. "I want to tell them who I am."

"I agree." She'd thought about nothing else since he'd walked into the house this morning. "They should hear the news from you."

"Really?" Both Walker and Brent seemed surprised by her immediate capitulation.

Hope lifted a shoulder. "I spoke with Dr. Stephens earlier this afternoon. Her advice was to tell the girls sooner rather than later, before they start asking questions."

"They haven't started asking questions?"

"Actually, they have. They want a father for Christmas." They'd meant Walker, but Hope didn't think that mattered as much as the truth. "You are the answer to their greatest wish."

Brent processed this in silence. "Did this Dr. Stephens give any advice on how I should tell them?"

"You need to keep it simple and direct."

"Simple and direct." He considered the advice. "Yeah, I can do that."

"I think I should be there when you tell them. Walker should be there, too." She looked at him for the first time since sitting down. "In case they don't respond well to the news."

Something passed between her and Walker, a silent agreement to be a united front. In that moment, Hope had a glimpse of what it would be like to have him in her life. The two of them acting as a single unit, the very essence of becoming a couple.

Did he feel it, too? She leaned toward him, wondering. Their connection had started with their mutual love of the twins. Somewhere along the way it had morphed into something more, something between just the two of them.

Brent's voice had her straightening in her chair. "You think the twins won't respond well to the news that I'm their father?"

"Honestly, I don't know."

For a moment, Brent looked devastated. But then he squared his shoulders and put on the face of a man determined to confront his past, and all that that implied. "Okay. If you think it's best that you and Walker be in the room when I tell them, then that's how we do it."

Chapter Sixteen

The following morning dawned as so many did in Colorado, without a cloud in the sky. The snow had stopped sometime in the middle of the night, leaving behind a blanket of fluffy white flakes. Hope lit the Christmas tree and, in the quiet stillness, stared at the twinkling lights. She hadn't slept well, too worked up over what the day held for the twins. Before the Evans brothers had called it a night, they'd agreed that Brent would tell the girls he was their father after their trip to see Santa.

Wishing it was over, Hope tidied up the room, moved a few decorations around, did some more tidying and…

She was procrastinating.

Determined to enjoy her time with the twins, she woke them and helped them into their prettiest dresses. Santa deserved their very best. Due to their excitement, the process took twice as long as it should have. Nevertheless, Hope prevailed before ushering them into the kitchen.

They were just finishing up breakfast when Walker and Brent arrived.

"They're here!" Harper squealed in delight.

Hope met the men at the door, the twins hard on her heels. Walker smiled at her and ping went her heart. They'd come so close to having a family together.

Walker bent low to greet the twins. They gave him a hug, then, seeing Brent, rushed over to him. He crouched in front of them. "Got a hug for me?"

Without a moment of hesitation, they dove for him.

Hope's breath caught at the sight of Brent's eyes filling with tears. Walker draped his arm over her shoulders and whispered, "It could be worse. They could dislike him."

"You're right."

Brent released the girls so they could show off their fancy dresses.

Once the fashion show came to a conclusion, Walker asked the twins. "Ready to meet Santa?"

They nodded vigorously.

Harper ran to Hope. She bent low as the little girl asked in a stage whisper, "Can Dr. Brent come with us to see Santa?"

"That's the plan."

"Yay!"

After a covert discussion, Walker and Hope agreed to let Brent stand in line with the twins. The excuse they gave the girls was that they wanted to take pictures. In reality, they were letting Brent build the trust he would need to tell them he was their father.

Putting his arm around her waist, Walker pulled Hope close.

Needing his strength, she leaned into him. "It hurts, letting them go."

"They're not gone yet."

They both knew that wasn't true. The girls adored their father already.

Stomach bottoming out, Hope glanced at Walker. He was looking rather worse for the wear, as if he'd had as rough a night as she had. The smile he gave her was full of warmth, and something new. There was a calmness about him that soothed her raw nerves. "We have some decisions to make, you and me."

"What about?"

Still smiling, he bent down to whisper in her ear, speaking what could either be a promise or a threat. "The future."

Two hours later, when they were back in his living room, Walker watched Hope set herself apart from the activity. She stood by the Christmas tree, gazing out the window, her eyes hooked on some unknown spot in the distance. Walker was the only one who noticed she'd retreated.

Brent sat on the overstuffed couch, bookended by his daughters. The twins kept up a running commentary about their time in Thunder Ridge. He did a respectable job keeping up with the conversation.

He was going to be a good father.

Walker wanted to be happy for his brother. But Brent's gain had come at too high a cost. Walker had taken a hit. Hope had taken a bigger one. In response, she'd put up a metaphorical wall. Walker didn't blame her, but he hated that she'd put him firmly on the outside with everyone else.

Brent took advantage of a lull in the conversation. "I have something to tell you girls."

This is it, Walker thought, glancing at Hope. The moment when he and Hope let go of a dream that had almost been theirs.

But this wasn't about them. It never had been.

They were here to support the twins. Together. Walker moved in next to Hope.

For an instant, she let down her guard and he saw his own sense of loss staring back at him. They'd come so close, only to lose the dream. Their shared sorrow was a living, breathing thing pulsing between them. He reached out and touched her arm. Her pain bled into his fingertips. The impact was like a physical blow.

He dropped his hand.

Walker shifted his attention to Brent and the twins.

They'd moved off the sofa. Brent had lowered to his knees, while the twins stood shoulder to shoulder facing him. Hands shaking, he touched each of their cheeks. "I have something very important to tell you."

Eyes solemn, Kennedy moved a step closer. Harper did the same. Father and daughters were united at last, but only one of them understood the gravity of the situation.

Walker was suddenly afraid for his brother. What if the twins didn't want him to be their father? What if this all went terribly wrong?

"Aunt Hope?" Kennedy's face took on a look of deep concern. "Why are you crying?"

Hope swiped her cheek. "I'm not crying. I just have something in my eye."

She laughed softly to make her point. There was something broken in the sound. Walker lifted a hand to comfort her. She moved out of his reach.

Brent gained the girls' attention again. "You know, I came to Thunder Ridge to meet you."

"You did?"

"Nothing could keep me away once I knew the

truth." He paused, drew in a deep breath and said in a quiet, calm voice, "I'm your father."

Two pair of eyes widened in shock. Harper recovered first. "You're our daddy?"

"I'm your daddy," Brent repeated, making his point so earnestly it was hard to disagree. "And you are my gorgeous daughters."

Through eyes that didn't seem to want to focus, Walker saw a watery version of father and daughters. The girls stared at Brent with identical expressions of wonder. Both looked so serious, poised to leap into his arms but not quite ready to do so yet.

They continued starting at him.

Brent stood still under his daughter's inspection, shaking slightly, so big and unsure of himself, shoulders hunched. Walker hurt for his brother. The expression on Brent's face was a combination of desperation and anxiety, as if he was in deep, unchartered waters and the girls were his personal life preservers.

Kennedy came out of her trance first. "Can we hug you?"

A muscle tightened in his jaw and then Brent's arms were open. "Get over here."

They launched themselves into the air. He caught them in a single swoop, clutching them against his chest and holding on for dear life. He didn't attempt to stop the tears from falling down his cheeks. And Walker felt like an intruder.

"We should leave them alone," he said in a hoarse whisper.

He was talking to empty air. Hope had already slipped out of the room. It took him five full minutes to find her. She was in his study, sitting at the desk he'd bought a few weeks after moving in. Her head was bent over the keyboard of her laptop, which was in the process of coming to life.

Something in her stiff posture warned him to tread carefully. "You left without a word."

Swiveling around, she looked at him for a long beat. "I didn't belong in the middle of that."

Turning away, she focused on her computer.

Walker wasn't afraid of much, but everything had been reduced to a dizzying moment of sheer panic when she opened the web browser and typed in the name of a popular airline. "What are you doing?"

"Checking for available flights back to New York."

No. She couldn't leave him. Forcing the panic out of his voice, he moved to stand beside her. "I thought we agreed no decisions until after the holidays."

"I'm looking for flights for December 26."

Two days. He only had two days to convince her to give him a chance, to give *them* a chance.

"Stay." He spun her chair around so he could speak to her face. "Hope. Please. Stay."

"I don't fit in here," she said in a halting voice. "I'm not one of you. I'm not one of anyone."

She was wrong. She was also not in the right frame of mind to hear his objections. "You can't abandon the twins." He knew it was a low blow. Desperation did that to a man. "They'll need you more than ever in the coming weeks."

Hope's shoulders slumped. "Maybe I'm more like my father than I want to admit."

"You know that's not true."

She whipped her head up to glare at him. "My first instinct is to run. All I want is to put distance between the girls and me, because staying is too painful."

Walker placed his hands on the sides of her chair. "Hope." He lowered in front of her. "Stay. At least through the New Year."

He could do a lot with an extra week. He could change the future. One week. That's all he needed. And a lot of prayer.

"The longer I remain in Thunder Ridge, the harder it will be for Brent to build a relationship with his daughters."

"That's absolutely untrue. Your presence will make the transition easier. No, don't shake your head at me. Listen. Just listen. You're the only stability the girls have known in a long time. They need you."

I need you.

She seemed to consider his words, but then she lowered her head and Walker could no longer see what was going on in her mind.

"Stay, Hope. If not for the twins, then for…" He hesitated only a moment before taking the biggest risk of his life since losing Rachel. "Us. Stay for us."

Her eyes moved to his face, and then away again. "We've only known each other a few weeks."

"Lifelong romances have started on less."

She gave an exasperated sigh.

"I know this thing between us seems to have happened fast because, well, it did happen fast. That doesn't make it any less real."

"Oh, Walker. I—"

"No, don't interrupt. Let me finish." Desperation made his voice gravelly. "All I'm asking is that you give me a chance to—"

His cell phone went off, the ringtone alerting him the call was from the hospital. Of all the rotten timing. "I have to take this. It's the hospital."

He listened for several seconds, then said in clipped tones. "On my way." He ended the call then shoved the phone in his pocket. "There's been a five-car pileup on the highway just outside of town. The ER is short-staffed due to the holidays. I have to go."

Her eyes went blank. "Of course you have to go."

Walker could see her pulling away from him, first emotionally, then physically as she swung back around to face her computer screen.

"I don't know how long I'll be gone," he said.

"I understand."

Unfortunately, Walker sensed her definition of *understanding* was not the same as his. He wanted to promise he'd be back soon, at least in time for the Christmas Eve service at church, but he couldn't know for sure. So he didn't make any promises. And realized his mistake as he watched Hope click on the airline's website for a one-way ticket to New York City.

"I'll be back. I promise."

She kept typing.

"Hope." He gripped the arm of the chair and swiveled her around to face him again. Before she could protest, he pulled her to her feet and straight into his arms. "Don't book that flight until I return."

She said nothing.

"Please." He kissed her then. And, wonder of wonders, she kissed him back. He continued kissing her like she was his.

She is mine, Walker realized. *She's my Hope.*

* * *

Several hours after Walker had left for the hospital, Hope stood by the cheerful Christmas tree, feeling anything but cheerful. Now that night had fallen, the lake was cast in an eerie blackness that matched her mood. She didn't think her heart could hurt any more than it already did, but as she thought back to the moment Walker had kissed her goodbye and then driven away in his SUV, she felt another fissure.

She'd never felt more alone in her life.

At the twins' insistence, Brent had walked with them over to Quinn's house. They wanted to tell the rest of the family their exciting news. Hope had been invited to tag along, but she'd opted to stay behind.

She wanted to curl up in a ball and hide from the world. She wanted to hop on a plane and never look back. For the first time in her life, Hope understood her father's choices. And with understanding came forgiveness. Reverend Jeffries had run from his pain.

Hope had nearly done the same thing.

But there was another way. She could stand and fight for what she wanted. Her life wouldn't look like what she'd thought three weeks ago, or even three days ago when she'd finalized the paperwork for her sabbatical from the university. But if she was very brave, she could reach for a new dream. And a new life. She could have the family she wanted. With Walker.

The sound of masculine footsteps quickened her pulse. He was home. Smiling, she spun around to face her future, only to feel her stomach bottom out. Brent had returned. And he was alone. "Where are the twins?"

"Playing with their cousins." He stopped, stuffed his hands in his pockets. "You and I need to talk."

Hope didn't want to have this discussion. "What do you want to talk about?"

"First, I want to tell you, again, how grateful I am you came looking for me."

Hope didn't want this man's gratitude. She didn't want to see the wonder in his eyes, or the joy of discovering a blessing he knew he hadn't earned. *He's not your enemy.*

Charity had wronged this man.

It helped to remember that Brent was as much a victim as the rest of them. That knowledge softened Hope's heart toward him. A little. Unfortunately, a shred of resentment remained. His gain was her loss. "Everything I've done in the past, and will do in the future, is for Harper and Kennedy."

"I know." He took her hand and gave her a grin reminiscent of his brother's. "Thank you for giving me the greatest gift of my life."

How could she hold a grudge against a man who understood the blessing he'd been given? "You're welcome."

"I'm going to do everything I can to be a good father to Harper and Kennedy. I promise."

She believed him. There would be several bumps along the way, and she would be here to help smooth them over. "I'm willing to work with you every step of the way."

"You're staying in Thunder Ridge?"

"I am." She told him about the year-long sabbatical she planned to take.

"A year isn't enough."

It wasn't. But that conversation was for her to have with Walker. In the meantime, she surprised them both by pulling him into a sisterly hug. "Welcome home, Brent."

"Thanks. So, listen." He stepped back a bit awkwardly. "If Walker doesn't make it home in time, I'd like you to join the family for the Evans traditional family Christmas Eve celebration."

"You want me to attend the church service with you?"

"Church is only one of the activities. Quinn throws a pretty amazing party, family only, which definitely includes you. So? What do you say? Will you join us?"

Under the circumstances, Hope could think of only one answer. "What time do we leave?"

Chapter Seventeen

The five-car pileup resulted in numerous injuries, some of them minor, others more serious and a few life-threatening. It had been a long night that had turned into a long morning. That had left Walker dead on his feet and more than a little worried he'd let Hope down.

He'd missed church. He also missed Quinn's Christmas morning breakfast, and several other family traditions. It was well after noon on Christmas Day before he pulled into his driveway. Exhausted and miserable, he was only partially relieved to see Hope's rental car parked in its usual spot. She hadn't left him. Yet.

She still could. She'd been pretty determined to run yesterday.

No way was he going to let her get away. And he planned to play dirty, pulling out all the stops as he breached the walls she'd built around her heart. The woman wouldn't know what hit her. If words failed him, or if Hope refused to give their relationship a shot, maybe the Christmas gift he'd picked up on his way home would change her mind.

Said gift released a loud yawn from the passenger seat. Walker patted the miniature version of Bertha on the head. He'd planned on giving Hope one of Daisy's puppies, but when he'd called Quinn during a short break last night, she'd informed him he was too late. The puppies were all spoken for, one of them by Brent. Walker smiled. The twins were getting both a father *and* a puppy for Christmas.

Thanks to another call, this one to Remy, the family's connection to all things furry, Walker had been able to find a decent solution to the problem. The Saint Bernard puppy was a better fit for Hope, anyway.

Feeling pretty good about himself, Walker picked up the sleepy animal and studied her face. "Hope is going to love you."

The puppy licked his chin.

Tucking the animal under his arm, Walker exited the car. He was barely halfway up the walkway when the front door swung open. Hope stood on the threshold, looking perfectly at home.

His feet ground to a halt. "You stayed."

Okay. Admittedly, it wasn't a great opening line.

She didn't seem to mind. Not if her smile was any indication. "I've been waiting for you for a very long time, Dr. Evans."

There was something underneath her words he couldn't quite identify. He was too overcome with relief to try. "The accident was a bad one, lots of injuries."

"No, you misunderstand." She crossed the distance between them. "I've been waiting for you all my life. And, now that I've found you, I'm not letting you go."

Walker nearly dropped the puppy. He held Hope's gaze, feeling the anxiety in his chest give way to anticipation. Could winning this amazing woman's heart be this easy? "Yeah?"

"Oh, yeah." Her gaze lowered to the squirming bundle under his arm. "Who's this handsome guy?"

"*She* is your Christmas present."

"Okay, wow." Hope touched one of the enormous paws, then the other. "I mean, wow. Our girl is going to be a monster."

"At least as big as Bertha." Walker swung the puppy forward and held her in the Simba pose so Hope could take a good look.

"Oh, Walker. You're killing me."

"There's more." He jiggled the puppy. "I have it on good authority, our girl is an old-fashioned dog at heart. She expects to grow up with both a mommy and daddy."

Hope took the puppy and pressed her face in the furry neck. When she looked back at him, her eyes were filled with tears. "What are we going to name her?"

We. Walker's heart swelled. "I was thinking we could let the twins do the honors."

"No way. They have their own puppy to name. This one's mine. Or rather—" she kissed the dog on the nose then hugged her close "—ours."

Caught in Hope's gaze, Walker's world tilted, wobbled a bit, then steadied. "I like the way you think, Dr. Jeffries."

"Come inside so I can give you your Christmas present."

The puppy fell asleep as soon as Hope set her on the rug near the Christmas tree. After giving the dog a few strokes, she retrieved a brightly wrapped Christmas present with a shiny red bow on top. "Open it."

Settled on the floor with Hope nestled in beside him, he tore away the paper, dug inside the box and discovered a framed photograph. He studied the image of him and Hope and the twins at the Ice Castles. They'd just arrived and were standing clustered together at the fountain, looking very much like a family.

"McCoy took the picture."

"I remember the day well." It had been one of the happiest of his life.

He felt a thread of pain over what might-have-been, but then came a spurt of joy. God hadn't provided Walker and Hope with the family they'd wanted. But they still had Harper and Kennedy in their lives.

And, now, they had each other.

"That, Walker Evans—" Hope tapped the photograph "—is the day I fell in love with you."

He kissed her, lingering a little longer than planned.

Hope pulled away, laughing softly. "I have one more gift to give you."

This time, when he unwrapped the box and lifted the lid, he discovered a bunch of torn-up scraps of paper. "I don't understand."

"You are holding the remains of the custody papers I had drawn up before I arrived in Thunder Ridge."

So Walker had been right to suspect her original motives. Hope had come to Thunder Ridge with the express idea of gaining full custody of the twins. "So this is your way of telling me you aren't going to sue for custody?"

She slid her fingers in his hair, smiled. "You're asking the wrong question."

"What question should I be asking?"

"It's not that I no longer plan to sue for custody, but rather *when* I made the decision to tear up the papers." She waved her hand in the general direction of the box.

"All right." He studied the box with a long considering look. "When did you tear them up?"

"The morning after the twins met your family." She sighed. "That's also when I put Plan B in place."

"Plan B?"

"I requested a one-year sabbatical from my job at the university."

Walker narrowed his eyes. "You were planning to stay in Thunder Ridge all along?"

"Not all along. Once I realized what you and your family could offer the girls, what I couldn't, I knew I wouldn't be taking them back to New York. But I also knew I couldn't live without them in my life, so I made plans to take the time to search for a teaching position closer to Thunder Ridge."

This woman's willingness to sacrifice for the people she loved would have brought Walker to his knees if he hadn't been sitting already. "That was a very brave thing to do."

She shrugged again. "I don't know about that. I never planned to fall in love with Thunder Ridge, or you, or your family, or—"

"Wait. Just wait a minute. That's the second time you've said you love me."

Hope blushed. "You caught that, huh?"

"I love you, too."

Her face broke out into a lovely smile, the one that never failed to reach inside his chest, grab his heart and squeeze. "Oh, Walker." Her smile slipped. "What about Rachel? Will you be able to let her—"

Walker cut her off with a kiss.

"Okay."

He took her face in his hands and kissed her again. "I won't pretend it wasn't hard letting Rachel go. Losing her nearly destroyed me. She'll always be in my heart. But she's my past. You are my future."

"I don't know if I can be second best in your heart."

His own heart melted at the pain he heard in her voice. How did he make her understand? By telling her the truth. "I hung on to Rachel entirely too long. I convinced myself I already had my one shot at happiness. God would never bless me with a second chance. Then you showed up and everything changed."

"Oh, Walker." She closed her eyes.

"Hope, look at me." When she did, he saw the tears. Felt answering ones well in his own eyes. "God has blessed me beyond what I deserve. He brought you into my life. I will not squander what we have. I will strive every day to be a man worthy of your love."

"You already are that man."

He pulled her close, kissed her, then whispered in her ear, "I could make this next part unnecessarily complicated for us both or I can make it simple."

"I like simple."

He slid to the floor, dropping to one knee.

"What…what are you doing?"

"I'm asking you to marry me." Taking her hand, he said, "But I should warn you, I don't have a ring yet."

"I don't need a ring."

"I should also tell you, I'm not a fan of long engagements."

"How long were you thinking?"

"A week."

She laughed. "Maybe we should consider a bit longer than that. After all, I'm not going anywhere."

And that was the biggest blessing of all.

"Hope Jeffries." He pressed a kiss to her palm. "Will you marry me?"

"Since we're keeping things simple…" Her smile lit the room. "Yes."

Epilogue

"Ten, nine, eight..."

Hope leaned into Walker and looked around Quinn's living room at the assembled group of family and friends. Her family now. Her friends. She gave herself permission to look her fill. Everyone had come dressed in casual clothing, another of the many Evans family traditions she already loved.

Hope's heart swelled to overflowing. God had blessed her with a life and a future far greater than she'd ever imagined.

"Seven, six..."

The Lord had brought her on a journey that had begun with fear and ended with certainty. For the first time in her life, Hope knew where she belonged. Here, in Thunder Ridge, Colorado. With the man of her dreams by her side.

"Five, four..."

She smiled into Walker's eyes. In silent agreement, they joined in the countdown. "Three." Walker grinned. "Two." Hope grinned right back. "One!"

"Happy New Year, Walker."

"Happy New Year, Hope."

Their lips met in an all-too-brief kiss before the twins separated them with giggles and enthusiastic words. "Happy New Year, Aunt Hope and Uncle Walker."

Lowering to their knees, they took turns embracing the girls.

A few more words, then off they went to find their father.

Hope sighed. She would miss Harper and Kennedy once they moved in with Brent. At least she had them a little while longer. They would stay with her in Walker's home until Brent found a suitable house for the three of them.

More change ahead. More upheaval. But one thing would remain steady. Her love for the twins. Family was, after all, family.

Walker pulled her close. "I have something for you."

Hope wasn't sure she could stand any more blessings. Her heart was already about to explode.

Walker's gaze roamed her features. "You know how much I love you, right?"

"I'm catching on to that, yes."

His hand dug into an interior pocket of his jacket. As if sensing something important was about to happen, everyone began gathering around them.

"I wanted to do this sooner," he said. "And would have. But tonight's gathering seemed the right time because everyone who matters is here with us."

Eyes locked with hers, he stepped around to face her directly. He held a square box covered in navy blue velvet in the tiny space between them.

Hope's hand flew to her mouth. "Is that what I think it is?"

"You tell me." With a flourish, he flipped open the lid.

Hope gasped at the sight of the three-stone diamond engagement ring with a white-gold setting that showed off the sparkling gems. "It's gorgeous."

He took her hand and slid the ring in place.

"It's a perfect fit, Walker."

"We're a perfect fit, Hope. You and me. Forever."

"Forever," she repeated.

He pulled her into his arms and kissed her.

A wild cheer went up from the crowd surrounding them.

Frowning, Walker glanced around, then turned back to Hope. "You don't mind I did this here?"

She smiled at him. "It was the exact right time and place."

Grinning, he pulled her back into his arms. "Welcome to the family, Hope. You're one of us now. For better or worse."

For better or worse.

She could live with that.

* * * * *

If you loved this story,
check out these other books

A Haven for Christmas
by Patricia Davids
An Amish Holiday Family
by Jo Ann Brown
The Rancher's Holiday Arrangement
by Brenda Minton
His Christmas Wish
by Allie Pleiter
The Christmas Bargain
by Lisa Carter

Available now from Love Inspired!

Find more great reads at
www.LoveInspired.com

Dear Reader,

Although this is my twentieth book with Love Inspired, I had as much fun guiding Hope and Walker to their happy ending as I did my first hero and heroine. I never tire of writing stories where two deserving people find love despite a few bumps along the way.

Every story I've written holds a place in my heart. But I confess there are some characters that stick with me long after I write The End. Hope and Walker fall into that category. There's something special about two wounded souls discovering a second chance at happiness. Walker and Hope didn't get the family they planned. But they found each other and a love that surpassed their previous heartaches. My kind of happy ending.

I have another confession to make. I'm a sucker for Christmas-themed romances. Add in a pair of five-year-old twins, puppies, a case of mistaken identity and—cue the happy dance.

I hope you enjoyed hanging out in Thunder Ridge. This was my first stop in town, but it won't be my last. In the meantime, I love hearing from readers. Let me know what kind of stories you prefer. You can contact me via

Get 4 FREE REWARDS!

We'll send you 2 FREE Books plus 2 FREE Mystery Gifts.

Love Inspired Suspense books showcase how courage and optimism unite in stories of faith and love in the face of danger.

FREE Value Over $20

COMING NEXT MONTH FROM
Love Inspired

Available December 1, 2020

AN AMISH HOLIDAY COURTSHIP
by Emma Miller

Ready to find a husband at Christmastime, Ginger Stutzman has her sights set on the handsome new Amish bachelor in town. But she can't help but feel drawn to her boss, Eli Kutz, and his four children. Could the widower be her true perfect match?

A PRECIOUS CHRISTMAS GIFT
Redemption's Amish Legacies • by Patricia Johns

Determined to find a loving Amish family for her unborn child, Eve Shrock's convinced Noah Wiebe's brother and sister-in-law are a great fit. But when she starts falling for Noah, the best place for her baby might just be in her arms...with Noah at her side.

HIS HOLIDAY PRAYER
Hearts of Oklahoma • by Tina Radcliffe

Beginning a new job after the holidays is the change widower Tucker Rainbolt's been praying for. Before he and his twin girls can move, he must ensure his vet clinic partner, Jena Harper, can take over—and stay afloat. But could giving his heart to Jena be the fresh start he *really* needs?

CHRISTMAS IN A SNOWSTORM
The Calhoun Cowboys • by Lois Richer

Returning home to his Montana family ranch, journalist Sam Calhoun volunteers to run the local Christmas festival. But as he works with single mom Joy Grainger on the project, the last thing he expects is for her children to set their sights on making him their new dad...

THE TEXAN'S UNEXPECTED HOLIDAY
Cowboys of Diamondback Ranch • by Jolene Navarro

Driven to get her sister and baby niece out of a dangerous situation, Lexy Zapata takes a job near Damian De La Rosa's family's ranch and brings them with her. Now they can stay hidden through Christmas, and Lexy will start planning their next move...if she can ignore the way Damian pulls at her heart.

A DAUGHTER FOR CHRISTMAS
Triple Creek Cowboys • by Stephanie Dees

Moving into a cottage on Triple Creek Ranch to help her little girl, Alice, overcome a traumatic experience, single mom Eve Fallon doesn't count on rescuing grumpy rancher Tanner Cole as he struggles to plan a party for foster kids. Can she revive both Tanner's and Alice's Christmas spirit?

LOOK FOR THESE AND OTHER LOVE INSPIRED BOOKS WHEREVER BOOKS ARE SOLD, INCLUDING MOST BOOKSTORES, SUPERMARKETS, DISCOUNT STORES AND DRUGSTORES.

LICNM1120